"Lin, you're not thinking straight."

"I'm not looking for forever." She placed her hand tentatively against his chest.

Though it pained him to do so, he grasped her hand and pulled it away before he did something irreversible. "You're not a fling sort of woman."

She looked up at him, and he saw a yearning in her eyes that was going to be damn hard to resist if he didn't get her back inside where his dad and Garrett could serve as a barrier.

"Maybe a fling is exactly what I need."

The woman was trying to kill him.

"I think we should go in."

"Why?" She took a deep breath. "We're both adults, Owen." She paused again before continuing. "Ones with needs."

He shook his head. "There are other ways to deal with those needs. Trust me."

Linnea lowered her gaze. "I'm sorry. I evidently read things wrong."

Her Cowboy Groom
TRISH MILBURN

First published in Great Britain 2015
by Mills & Boon, an imprint of Harlequin (UK) Limited,
Large Print edition 2015
Eton House, 18-24 Paradise Road,
Richmond, Surrey, TW9 1SR

© 2015 Trish Milburn

ISBN: 978-0-263-25997-1

Harlequin (UK) Limited's policy is to use papers that are natural, renewable and recyclable products and made from wood grown in sustainable forests. The logging and manufacturing processes conform to the legal environmental regulations of the country of origin.

Printed and bound in Great Britain
by CPI Antony Rowe, Chippenham, Wiltshire

TRISH MILBURN

writes contemporary romance for the Mills & Boon® American Romance line and paranormal romance for the Harlequin Nocturne series. She's a two-time Golden Heart Award winner, a fan of walks in the woods and road trips, and a big geek girl, including being a dedicated Whovian and Browncoat. And from her earliest memories, she's been a fan of Westerns, be they historical or contemporary. There's nothing quite like a cowboy hero.

To all the lovely readers who have written to me about enjoying the Blue Falls, Texas series and asking when the next book will be out. That's music to a writer's ears. Thanks from the bottom of my heart for your interest and continued support.

Chapter One

Linnea Holland only had five minutes before opening time for her bridal boutique and a busy day of catering to the romantic dreams of Dallas brides-to-be. Still, that was enough time for one more peek.

She hurried to the back of the building, to the room that held the most gorgeous wedding gown Linnea had ever seen. And it was hers. In two weeks, she would wear the Ellen Clare original design as she walked down the aisle toward her very own prince.

Okay, so Michael wasn't an actual prince, but he certainly treated her like a queen. The past six months together had been a whirl-wind of fancy dinners in fine restaurants, beau-tiful flower bouquets delivered to her at the store when he had to go out of town on busi-ness and an engagement ring that had taken her breath away. As she stood and stared at the dress with lace so delicate it looked as if it might float away into mist if she touched it, she still couldn't believe she was going to be Mrs. Michael Benson. Sometimes she pinched her-self to make sure she wasn't in the longest, most realistic dream imaginable.

Not only was Michael a successful executive with a big investment firm and drop-dead gor-geous, but somehow out of all the women he could have, he'd chosen her, the middle daugh-ter of two teachers. And it had all started when she accidentally bumped into him coming out of a coffee shop, dousing his crisp white shirt and designer suit with a caramel latte. She'd been mortified, and he'd asked her out on the spot, stunning her speechless. He'd just smiled until she'd remembered how to utter a "Yes."

It had been the kind of first meeting you saw in movies, and the moment he asked her to marry him she'd been determined to make her wedding like something out of a fairy tale.

She glanced at the clock and hurried out of the room. She might have a fairy-tale wedding on the horizon, but until then she had a business to run. She reached the front door just as she heard Katrina, her business partner, coming in the back.

"Sorry I'm late," Katrina called out.

Linnea turned the lock on the door, then headed toward the curved white counter in the middle of the store. "You're not late."

"Well, late for me," Katrina said as she shoved her purse into a drawer behind the counter.

Linnea smiled at Katrina. "Considering you're here at least half an hour early every day, I think one day of right on time isn't going to mar your record."

The truth was, Linnea couldn't have asked for a better partner in her business. Katrina possessed a lot of business savvy, loved the boutique as much as Linnea did and was an excellent salesperson. Michael liked to tease them by calling them the odd couple because Katrina was petite with a stylish black bob, while Linnea stood several inches taller and had long, wavy red hair. They might look different, but in all the ways that mattered they were a perfect business match.

"So, how many times have you been back to stare at your dress this morning?" Katrina asked before taking a drink of her coffee.

"Only once."

Katrina laughed a little. "Going into withdrawal yet?"

Linnea bumped Katrina's shoulder with her own. Before she could think of an appropriate response, however, their first appointment of the day arrived— Rena Cavendish and her very demanding mother. Linnea put on her best smile and went to work.

By the time Rena's mother finally agreed on the last of the details for her daughter's wedding, Linnea felt as if she needed about twelve hours of sleep to recuperate. Still, she didn't let her smile waver as the Cavendish women made their departure. It was her job to make them happy, to make them believe helping them was the absolute highlight of her day. Most of the time, she did love every minute of her job. But there was the occasional mother like Marilyn Cavendish or a true bridezilla who made keeping her smile from faltering extra challenging.

When Rena and Marilyn disappeared around the corner, Linnea felt like massaging her aching facial muscles. She glanced across the store to where Katrina was aiding a young bride who, by contrast, was as sweet as pie.

The door chime drew Linnea's attention. A woman perhaps a few years older than her with blond hair pulled back in a chignon walked in.

"Good morning," Linnea said, smiling more naturally this time. "How can I help you?"

"You're Linnea Holland." The fact that the words weren't a question left Linnea with an odd feeling. Maybe it was the way the woman was staring at her without looking away.

"Yes. I'm sorry, have we met?"

"You're engaged to Michael Benson?"

Linnea searched for a reason for the strange conversation. "I am. Do you know Michael?"

"You're going to want to call off that wedding."

Linnea jerked back a bit at the woman's words and what seemed like anger barely banked below the surface. "And why would I do that?"

"Because he's already married. To me."

Linnea gripped the edge of the counter to steady herself. Before she realized Katrina had moved away from the customer she was helping, she was there next to Linnea, placing a comforting hand on her arm.

"Ma'am, what is the meaning of this?" Katrina said softly to shield her words from the young bride-to-be.

A glance in that direction, however, told Linnea that the unexpected conversation had not gone unnoticed.

The woman also looked toward the customer. The latter held a wedding gown in front of her as she looked in the mirror and failed to do a very convincing job of pretending she wasn't listening to them. Shifting her gaze back to Linnea, the woman claiming to be Michael's wife stepped closer.

"Listen, I'm not accusing you of husband stealing or anything."

"Good, because I'm not," Linnea said with more than a little heat in her response. She wanted this woman and her crazy accusations to go away.

The sympathy that appeared in the other woman's eyes scared Linnea more than anything she'd said.

"My name is Danielle Benson. Michael and I have been married for six years."

Linnea shook her head. "No, you're wrong."

"I assure you I'm not." Danielle pulled a photo out of her purse and placed it atop the counter.

Linnea's breath caught as she stared down at a photo of Michael, a little younger, in a tux and holding the hands of the woman who now stood in front of Linnea. The younger version of Danielle wore a wedding gown and was looking up at Michael as if she couldn't believe she'd gotten so lucky. Linnea knew that feeling. Again, she shook her head. "Photos are remarkably easy to manipulate."

Danielle patted her purse. "I have a copy of our marriage license."

"All that would prove is that you were married at one point." Sure, Michael had said nothing about being married before, but she needed to believe that if he ever had been he was now divorced. The alternative was just too horrible to be believed. Her Michael wouldn't do something like that.

"I know this is hard to hear, and trust me when I tell you that it isn't any easier to say. I didn't want to believe my husband was cheating on me, but when I found out that he was actually planning to marry someone else, someone who had no idea he was already married… Well, I knew I couldn't let him hurt you like he has me."

"No, this can't be right. You're mistaken. There are probably lots of Michael Bensons." Even as Linnea tried to explain away Danielle's claims, doubt began to seep in like water finding the cracks in a rock. There might be a lot of Michael Bensons, but they didn't look like her Michael. Linnea's hearing seemed to fade, and the world around her started to spin in nauseating circles as Danielle explained how she'd hired a private investigator to follow Michael and that the PI was the one who'd relayed that Linnea was totally unaware of Michael's marital status.

In the blink of an eye, the meager contents of Linnea's stomach staged a revolt that sent her racing for the bathroom. She slammed the door behind her and made it to the toilet just in time. After she finally stopped retching, she found she didn't have the strength to push herself up from the floor. And then the tears came.

She needed to call Michael, to straighten this mess out. But as she sat on the floor in her favorite teal pencil skirt, doubts and questions began to peck at her like the beaks of sinister birds. The fact that she'd never met Michael's parents, how he'd never taken her to any company function and all the long business trips. She strangled on a sob when she considered those trips hadn't been for business at all but that he'd been going home to his wife.

A knock on the door was followed by Katrina's voice. "Are you okay?"

No, she wasn't okay. She might never be okay again.

When Linnea didn't answer, Katrina opened the door.

"Oh, hon." Katrina kneeled beside her and pushed an errant lock of hair back behind Linnea's shoulder. "I'm so sorry."

Linnea met her friend's gaze. "You believe her?"

The sympathy on Katrina's face, different from Danielle's but no less devastating, caused Linnea's insides to twist into painful knots. "Is she still here?"

"No, she left."

"Please bring me my phone."

"Don't you think you should give yourself a few minutes?"

"No. I need to know the truth now."

Katrina left and returned a few moments later with the phone. Linnea's hands were shaking so much she nearly fumbled the phone right into the toilet.

"You want me to dial for you?"

Linnea shook her head. Katrina knew her well enough that she stepped out of the bathroom, leaving Linnea alone. Linnea closed the door and somehow managed to dial Michael's cell number. She didn't think she'd be able to handle it if she got his voice mail, but part of her dreaded talking to him, too.

"Hey there," he answered, startling her. "How's my favorite girl?"

A surge of pure anger raced through her veins. "I just met your wife."

Please deny it. Please say it isn't true, that Danielle is a crazy woman.

But as moments passed without a response from Michael, Linnea's heart broke completely in two. Her dreams shattered around her like exploding glass.

"Linnea—"

She ended the call before he could say anything else. Just the tone of his voice as he said her name told her all she needed to know. He'd been lying to her for months, from the moment he met her. And she'd fallen for it, every last word.

She had no idea how much time passed as she sat on the bathroom floor, too stunned to move. Every minute she'd spent with Michael, every conversation they'd shared, every promise he'd made with loving words—she went back over all of it, searching for some clue that she was being duped. How could she have been so blind?

A gentle knock on the door was followed by

Katrina poking her head in. "Is there anything I can do to help?"

Linnea just stared at her friend, unable to form a response.

"Why don't you go home?" Katrina said. "I'll handle things here."

Something about those words finally penetrated Linnea's mind enough that she found the strength to push herself to her feet. "No, I'll be out in a minute."

Katrina looked as if she might argue, but instead she gave a small nod and left Linnea alone again.

Linnea brushed her teeth and rinsed out her mouth. She smoothed her hair and took a deep breath that did little to fortify her. Still, she wasn't going to let Michael rob her of anything else, certainly not the joy she derived from her job.

But as she walked out into the showroom filled with stunning white gowns, ethereal veils and all manner of happily ever after, it all suddenly felt like a bigger lie than the ones Michael had told.

She placed her hand against the roiling in her stomach. "I think I will go home." Needing to get away as fast as she could, she grabbed her purse and raced for her car.

Her phone rang as she crossed the parking lot. When she saw Michael's name, she ignored the call. He called back almost immediately and again as she was driving home. To keep from tossing her phone out the window, she turned it off and shoved it deep into her purse.

When she pulled into the parking space in front of her condo, she couldn't remember how she'd gotten there. Her bottom lip quivered, her fragile hold on her emotions threatening to disintegrate. Through some miracle of self-control, she made it inside before the fresh wave of tears would no longer be denied. On wobbly legs, she barely made it to the couch before the silent tears turned into heart-rending sobs.

LINNEA WOKE SLOWLY to realize she must have cried herself to sleep. The angle of the sun indicated it was sometime after noon. The throbbing in her head and the fact that her eyes were itchy with dried tears told her the horrible events of the morning hadn't just been a nightmare.

She lay there staring at the dust motes floating in the beam of sunlight coming through the window. Part of her wanted to go back to sleep, but she knew it wouldn't help her feel any better. It wasn't going to make the truth go away. She pushed herself to a sitting position and wondered how she was going to break the news to her parents, her sisters, her friends. How did she tell all of them that her fairy tale was nothing but a cruel lie?

Anger welled up inside her, competing for

space with the pain gnawing away at her. Why would Michael do this? Had he truly never cared about her? About his wife?

There was nothing she wanted more in that moment than to be done with all the hard conversations. Actually, what she wanted even more was to run away from her life. How could she go back to peddling the dream of wedded bliss when hers had been snatched away in the most awful way possible?

Knowing that breaking the news wasn't going to get any easier if she waited longer, she dug her phone out of her purse and turned it on. The screen revealed she had a dozen missed calls. She listened to one from Katrina asking if she needed anything, but the ten calls from Michael she deleted without listening to them. Nothing he could say could make her forgive him for breaking her heart and making a complete fool out of her. The other call was from Chloe, her best friend since they'd roomed together in college, the woman who was supposed to be her matron of honor.

"Hey, Lin. Just calling to finalize some details." In the midst of the call, Chloe suddenly laughed. She sounded as if she'd pulled the phone away from her mouth when she said, "Cut it out." Next came a distinctively male chuckle, no doubt Chloe's new husband, Wyatt. Linnea's heart squeezed at the sound of her friend so happy and in love, even if she was scolding her husband. "Sorry about that," Chloe continued. "Call me when you get a chance."

Linnea deleted the message as if it would erase the sounds of marital bliss, as well. She was happy that Chloe had found a good man to love and be loved by, truly she was. At least she hoped Wyatt was everything he claimed to be, not like Michael and his web of lies.

She shook her head, not wanting to let what had happened turn her into someone who was suspicious of every man in the world. After all, she knew deep down there were lots of good guys like her father, like Chloe's dad.

She scrolled to her parents' number, but she couldn't make herself hit the Call button. Her mother had been just as excited about the wedding as Linnea, if not more so. The news that Michael wasn't who he'd seemed to be would break her mother's heart, too.

Deciding to wait awhile longer to make that call, she instead forced herself to dial Chloe's number. Better to test out her ability to share the news on her best friend instead of risking turning into a blubbering mess on the phone with her mother. Her mom would no doubt rush right over to wrap her baby in her arms when Linnea just wanted to be left alone. The last thing she wanted was to look into anyone else's eyes and see the pity she'd detected in Katrina's.

Her fingers shook as she hit Chloe's number,

and she bit her bottom lip to keep from crying again.

"Hey," Chloe answered. "I was beginning to think you were ignoring me."

Despite her best efforts, a tear broke free and ran down Linnea's cheek. "No, I… It's just been a bad day." She sniffed against a fresh rush of tears.

"Lin, what's wrong?"

"The wedding's off," she said, her voice shaking.

"Off? What happened?" The sound of a closing door came through the phone.

"Michael is…" She stopped to swallow against the large lump clogging her throat as if she'd swallowed a lemon whole. "He's already married."

She struggled to share everything that had happened that morning with Chloe. By the time she was finished, hot, salty tears were streaming down her face again, burning trails in her skin like lava flows.

"Lin, I don't know what to say. 'I'm sorry' is not enough."

Linnea swiped at another tear. "I feel so hollow inside, and I have no idea how I'm going to go back to work and pretend I'm happy. Nobody will buy a wedding gown from someone who is wearing a broken heart on her sleeve."

"Come here."

"What?"

"There's a free bedroom at the ranch now since I moved out, and Dad, Garrett and Owen are away from the house most of the day. No one will bother you there. You won't have to smile and pretend."

This was why she loved Chloe so much. She understood her, often better than her own family did. "Thanks for the offer, but I've got so much to take care of here. Things to cancel, a business to run."

"That's why they make phones and computers and business partners."

As much as she wanted to run away, she couldn't. She had responsibilities, and she didn't want Michael to know how badly he'd hurt her. She had to be strong, no matter how much it hurt.

Banging on the front door startled her.

"Linnea, let me explain," Michael shouted through the door.

"Thanks for listening, Chloe, but I need to make some more calls."

"It's a standing invitation. You are welcome here anytime, for however long you need."

Fresh tears popped into Linnea's eyes, these because despite everything she was lucky to have the absolute best friend in the world.

Michael knocked again. "I'm not leaving until you talk to me."

The last thing she wanted to do was look into his deceitful eyes and listen to more lies fall from his lips. So she ignored him and went up to her bedroom. For a long time, she feared he was going to live up to his promise that he wouldn't leave until he talked to her. But after a little more than an hour, she watched as he drove away.

Chloe's words echoed in her head as she made her way down to the kitchen and looked in her fridge for something to eat. But as she stood staring at the contents of her refrigerator, nothing looked appealing. Even though her body was hungry, she couldn't imagine anything tasting good. So she closed the door and leaned back against it.

She wandered from room to room as if she might find peace and a release from the pain in one of them. When she found herself in her bedroom again, she sank onto the side of the bed and realized she couldn't put off telling her family the news any longer. She didn't want to risk her mom or one of her sisters stopping by the store and finding out something was wrong from Katrina.

After forcing herself to take several slow, deep breaths, she hit the number for her parents' house.

"Hey, sweetie," her mom answered. "I was just about to call you and see if you wanted to have lunch with Heather and me. We're going shopping for the baby afterward, if you think you could pry yourself away from work for a while."

Linnea's lip trembled again at the idea of being around that much happiness when her world was falling apart. Not only had her older sister, Heather, been married to a great guy for two years, but they were expecting their first baby around Thanksgiving. A mere three months separated Linnea from becoming an aunt for the first time, but today the thought only made her want to cry. She'd dreamed of having a bundle of joy to call her own, as well, but now…

"I'm sorry, Mom. I'm not up for lunch today."

"What's wrong? I can hear something's wrong in your voice."

Linnea wanted to believe that the telling of what had happened would be easier the second time through, but she was wrong. It was so much worse.

"Oh, honey. I'll be right over."

"No, I'm fine."

"You don't have to pretend to be brave. You're my daughter, and I intend to be there for you."

Desperation filled Linnea to overflowing. She loved her mom dearly, was thankful she had caring parents who were always there for their children when they needed them. But for some reason, her mom had never grasped that when Linnea said she wanted to be alone, she actually meant it.

"I won't be here. I'm going to visit Chloe for

a few days." She hadn't meant to take Chloe up on her offer, but the words had flown out of her mouth before she'd even thought about them. But now that she'd committed, it felt right. She could give herself a few days to get over the shock, to make all the necessary calls to cancel her fantasy wedding, to prepare herself for going back to the work of encouraging customers to buy in to the dream of forever.

"Honey, are you sure?"

"Positive." And she realized it was true.

When she finally promised her mother that she'd call if she needed her for anything, anything at all, and agreed to let her mother make some of the necessary cancellation calls, Linnea tossed a few items of clothing and toiletries in a bag, grabbed her laptop and hurried for her car. She didn't think she breathed until she drove out of her neighborhood and away from the chance that either her mother or Michael might show up at her front door.

She pointed her car toward Blue Falls, the small town in the Hill Country that Chloe called home. It might not be Linnea's home, but right now the familiar was the last thing she needed. If she had only one wish, it would be that Blue Falls held some magical way of making her forget Michael Benson and the giant hole he'd left where her heart should be.

Chapter Two

"Come on back to my place," Tiffany Clark whispered into Owen Brody's ear as she clung to him like a barnacle. "You know you want to."

Part of him was tempted by her curvy figure and her warm lips nibbling on his ear. Plenty of times he would have taken her up on it. But tonight he was just dog tired after a day of working on the ranch with his brother and dad and then a couple of hours devoted to training the horse he hoped would make a good roping horse. And then he'd gotten the bright idea to come into town for a couple of beers and to scope out the female landscape at the dance hall. Halfway into his first beer, he wished he'd stayed home and gone to bed.

Now, if that wasn't a sad statement about his life. It wasn't as if he was an old codger, but for some reason his normal routine of working hard followed by playing hard just wasn't doing it for him tonight.

He gently pushed Tiffany away from him. "Not tonight, Tiff. I'd be falling in my plate if I had a plate."

His rebuff earned him a pout from Tiffany, and for a moment he reconsidered passing on the pleasure she was offering. But he had the oddest feeling that his being tired wasn't the only reason he wasn't dragging Tiffany and her tasty curves to the nearest bed. Hell, the nearest horizontal surface. But damned if he knew why she didn't look quite as appealing as she once had.

Owen slipped off the bar stool where he was sitting and tossed a couple of bills on the bar.

"Calling it a night so soon?" asked James Turner, who was tending bar tonight.

"Yeah, just hit the wall."

James shot him a crooked grin. "I think hell just froze over."

"Be careful or I'll take my tip back."

James just laughed and moved to fill another drink order.

Owen stepped out of Tiffany's reach before she could attach herself to him again and made for the door. He stifled a yawn as he headed out the door and across the parking lot to his truck. A stiff breeze sent a paper cup tumbling across the parking lot, and thunder rumbled in the distance, promising some good sleeping weather.

As he drove toward home, a few sprinkles of rain began to fall. Just as he passed Crider Road, he noticed emergency flashers blinking on a car up ahead. As he got closer, he spotted a small silver car pulled halfway off the road. A woman wearing a skirt and high heels stood beside the car and then proceeded to kick the flat rear tire. He couldn't help but chuckle at the image she made even though she was obviously upset.

He pulled in behind her and parked, leaving his headlights on to illuminate her and the car as he slipped out of the truck.

"I don't think that's going to help," he said as hc approached her.

When she looked toward him, he hesitated for a moment as recognition hit. "Linnea? What are you doing out here?"

She took a step back as she shaded her eyes against the bright light. He realized she must have figured out she wasn't in the safest position, broken down alone on the side of a rural road at night.

"It's Owen Brody. Are you headed to the ranch?"

She seemed to deflate more than relax. "That

was the plan, but my tire had a different idea." She sounded even more drained than he felt.

He walked the rest of the distance to the rear of her car. "Don't worry. I'll get this changed for you."

"Thank you." Her voice sounded so small that he met her eyes and saw a sadness there that he'd never seen before in his sister's best friend.

"You okay?"

"Been a rough day."

He wasn't a "share your feelings" sort of guy, but for some reason he wanted to ask her what was wrong. Instead, he asked her to pop the car's trunk so he could get the spare before the approaching storm reached them.

She moved to comply and had to catch herself against the side of the car when she twisted her ankle off the edge of the pavement. The curse that came from her shocked Owen, it being so at odds with the classy lady he'd always known her to be.

"Did you hurt yourself?"

"I'm fine."

She sounded anything but fine, but he wasn't going to push. He knew better than to wave the proverbial red flag in front of a woman already in a foul mood.

When the trunk latch disengaged, he opened the lid and found the spare tire, one of those little donut deals. "Hate to tell you this, but your spare is as flat as a pancake, too."

"Of course it is." Linnea bit her lip and lifted her gaze to the darkened sky just as the raindrops picked up their pace.

He closed the trunk. "Come on. I'll give you a ride to Chloe's. We'll get your tires fixed in the morning."

"I…I was actually going to your house."

He looked at her, growing more confused by the moment.

"I'm sorry," she said as she shook her head. "I should have called her back. She offered me the extra room for a few days, but I see she didn't tell you all about it. If you could give me a ride into town, I'll get a room at the inn."

When had his house become his sister's bed-and-breakfast? Although he had to admit Linnea was a lot nicer to look at than the last guest they'd had. Not that Wyatt wasn't a decent-enough-looking guy, but he was a guy. They already had enough testosterone and stinky socks around without adding more.

"Don't be silly," he said. "Come on before you get soaked."

Linnea hesitated before opening the back door and grabbing a couple of bags and her purse. As she started toward him, he saw her wince when she put weight on her twisted ankle. He'd never liked seeing a woman in pain, so he stepped up beside her and wrapped his arm around her waist, taking some of her weight.

She stiffened for a moment before allowing her muscles to relax a little. "Thanks."

"No thanks necessary. Rescuing damsels in distress, it's what I do."

He expected a laugh, a smile, something. But when she offered none of those, he realized this was not the same Linnea who'd been texting Chloe pictures of wedding stuff for months. Someone who was as happy as Linnea supposedly was about her upcoming marriage didn't look as if someone had run over her dog and then laughed about it. But it wasn't his business. Female drama was Chloe's department.

As the rain picked up its pace, he ushered her toward the driver's-side door of his truck. "It'll be easier for you to get in over here. Can't have you toppling into the ditch."

She made an attempt to smile at him this time, but damned if it didn't look shaky and as if she might dissolve into tears at any moment. Oh, hell. He so didn't do tears. He had to get to the ranch and hand her off to his sister. As she slid across the truck to the passenger side, he sent a quick text to Chloe to get her butt over to his house because he'd just picked up her best friend on the side of the road.

By the time they reached the house, the rain was coming down in slanting sheets. He parked but didn't get out of the truck. Part of him wanted to curse that he hadn't taken Tiffany up on her offer. A woman who had a night of naughtiness on her mind—that he could deal with. Sitting in a truck with a woman who looked on the verge of tears as the heavens unloaded on them? Not so much.

His phone buzzed with a text from his sister. "Chloe says she'll be here as soon as the rain lets up."

"She doesn't have to get out in this." Linnea shook her head. "I should have just stayed at home."

Yeah, something was definitely wrong in happily-ever-after land. Knowing he was going to kick himself for asking, he did anyway. "What's wrong?"

He thought she wasn't going to answer at first, but then she took a shaky breath. "I'm not getting married after all."

Oh, hell, why had he opened his big mouth?

Linnea shifted her gaze out the window, through the stream of water running down the other side of the glass. "Turns out I was engaged to someone who was already married."

He cursed, couldn't help it. He searched for the appropriate thing to say, but came up empty save for a weak "Sorry."

"Me, too."

Part of him was curious, but he wasn't digging himself deeper into this emotional hole. Instead, he hopped out into the rain that had slackened a fraction and hurried around to her side of the truck. He opened the door and helped her out and hurried with her to the porch. He made sure she was safely up the steps before he ran back to the truck for her bags.

When he reached the porch, he found her standing there waiting for him, her arms wrapped around her wet body, her hair dripping. Despite the fact that it was early September in Texas, he had the strongest urge to wrap her in a blanket to make sure she didn't catch a chill.

Reminding himself that Linnea was a grown woman and perfectly capable of taking care of herself, flat tires notwithstanding, he opened the door and motioned for her to precede him inside.

It wasn't until he followed her that he realized he should have gone first. Luckily, his dad and Garrett were kicked back watching TV, but one of them could just as easily have been strolling through the living room in his underwear. He didn't think Linnea needed to be assaulted with that image, even if she hadn't just had the worst day ever.

"Linnea?" Wayne Brody got to his feet. Before he could say anything else, Owen shook his head a little where Linnea couldn't see him. He saw acknowledgment in his dad's eyes before his dad crossed the living room and gave Linnea a hug. "It's good to see you."

Linnea pulled out of his arms. "I'll get you all wet."

His dad laughed. "Honey, I don't think a few raindrops are going to do me in."

Owen lifted Linnea's bag a little higher. "You want to change into something dry?"

Linnea met his eyes for a moment, then nodded. "Thanks." She took the bag and headed for Chloe's old room.

No one said anything until the door clicked closed.

"What's going on?" Garrett asked from where he'd sunk onto the arm of the couch.

Owen kept his voice low so Linnea wouldn't hear. "Chloe told Linnea she could stay here for a few days, but they got their wires crossed somehow. I found Linnea on the side of the road with a flat tire."

"Why would she want to stay here?" his dad asked. "She and Chloe got wedding stuff to do or something?"

Owen glanced toward the hallway to make sure Linnea was still in the bedroom. "She said the wedding is off."

"Off?"

Owen shrugged. "That's what she said."

"And Chloe thought the best place for her was here?" Garrett asked.

"I guess 'cause there's an extra bedroom here. At Chloe's she'd have to sleep on the couch."

"And have to see happy newlyweds, the last thing she probably wants to see right now," Wayne said.

So maybe Linnea staying in the extra room

here did make more sense. A heads-up would have been nice, though.

After Owen went to change out of his own wet clothes, he noticed that Linnea hadn't come out of the bedroom. Had she fallen asleep? Or was she just hiding? He had no idea what to do, if he was supposed to do anything. Maybe the best thing was to just leave her alone, let Chloe take care of things when she got here. But from the sound of the rain, that might be a while.

The living room sat empty when he walked back in. He found his dad in the kitchen pulling a bowl of hot chili out of the microwave. Beyond him in the utility room, Garrett was shoving a load of dirty clothes into the washing machine.

"Here, take this to Linnea," Wayne said as he added a sleeve of crackers and a spoon to the wooden tray, part of a set Chloe had gotten them last Christmas for when they ate in front of the TV during football games.

"Me?"

Wayne cocked an eyebrow. "Yeah, she doesn't bite."

But what if she was in the bedroom crying? "Shouldn't we just leave her alone until she's ready to come out?"

"She might not come out tonight. And chances are if she's upset she hasn't eaten."

Owen bit down on the urge to ask why his dad didn't take the chili to Linnea, instead grabbing the tray. Might as well get it over with. When he reached the guest room, he held the tray in one hand while he knocked on the door with the other. He heard movement inside before Linnea opened the door. Thank God she didn't look as if she'd been crying, at least not recently. But there was evidence of earlier tears in the puffiness around her eyes.

"Dad warmed up some chili for you."

"He didn't have to do that."

"Wasn't a problem. We tend to make enough to feed half of Texas when we cook chili."

Linnea smiled a little as she reached out and took the tray. "Thank you."

After an awkward moment, he nodded and started to walk away.

"Owen?"

He looked back at her. The unsure hesitance on her face was so unlike Linnea. She was usually full of life and buzzing around like a bee, always doing something. She and Chloe had been the perfect college roommates. Seeing her look broken and sad left him with the most helpless feeling he'd had in a very long time.

"Thanks, for everything. I'll get out of your hair as soon as I can get the tire fixed."

While part of him had no idea what to do with a heartbroken woman in his house, he got the oddest feeling that maybe she was just where she needed to be at the moment.

"Don't worry about it. The room is just sitting

here empty. If you can stand being around us, you're welcome to stay. You class up the joint."

When she offered him the hint of a smile, it made him happier than it should.

LINNEA KNEW SHE should leave the bedroom and be social, especially since she'd dropped in on the Brody men unannounced. But she just couldn't make herself do it. She feared she'd lose her tenuous grip on her control and start crying in front of them. And despite the fact that they'd been around Chloe for years, she doubted they knew how to deal with an overly emotional female. No, it was better if she just stayed out of sight for a while. In fact, she texted Chloe that there was no need for her to get out in the rain even though the house she shared with Wyatt was only a few miles away on another part of the ranch. She'd just talk to her the next day, when hopefully Linnea would have more control over her heartbreak.

She didn't feel much like eating, but her stomach had other ideas. It was empty and demanding to be fed. She'd not eaten anything since breakfast, and honestly she was a little lightheaded from lack of food. So she sat in the comfortable reading chair in the corner and took a bite of the chili. She thought she'd only be able to manage a few spoonfuls, but she ended up emptying the bowl and half the sleeve of crackers.

Linnea felt no better about the state of her life, but at least she wasn't hungry on top of that.

The minutes ticked by at an agonizingly slow pace. She was beginning to think coming to the ranch had been a very bad idea. Maybe she should have gone somewhere no one knew her like the beach, on a cruise, the other side of the world.

Her phone buzzed, drawing her out of a daydream about lying in the sun in the Caribbean.

When she saw that it was Michael, her bottom lip quivered. She wouldn't have thought it possible, but her heart broke into even more pieces. How many times had seeing his name on her phone display made her smile? Sent joy coursing through her heart? Too many to count. But now it just made her want to crush the phone in her hand until it was nothing but dust. With her fingers shaking, she blocked his number. And then the tears started to fall again.

She curled into the bed and covered her head with a pillow, hoping it muffled the sound enough that no one would hear her. Having an unexpected guest drop in was bad enough. But having that guest turn into a blubbering mess was even worse.

Still, she couldn't help it. She'd thought putting distance between her and Michael would be a good thing, but she actually felt worse. And she couldn't contain the hurt anymore, so she let it flow out as quietly as she could when what she really wanted to do was scream and wail and ugly cry until there was nothing left inside her.

Linnea fell asleep with her clothes on and the tears still flowing. When she woke the next morning, she realized it was because she heard Owen, Garrett and their dad getting ready to head out to work. Judging by how she felt, she knew she had to be quite a sight with her puffy, itchy eyes, stuffy nose and pounding headache. And her body ached as if she'd been body-slammed.

She lay in the bed staring at the ceiling as footsteps came down the hall, then paused for a moment outside her door before moving on. Was it Owen? His dad? Owen had always been the wildest of the Brody clan, according to Chloe, moving from job to job and never one to turn down an opportunity to have a good time. But the night before, he'd acted more like his sister, caring and offering a helping hand.

Maybe she'd looked as fragile as she'd felt, and he'd been afraid she'd break.

After the house grew quiet, she still couldn't force herself out of bed. She hated feeling so miserable, so pathetic, but she just couldn't muster the energy to move.

Several minutes later, she heard a door open and close and wondered if one of the guys had forgotten something. But then there was a light knock on her door.

"Lin? You awake?" Chloe asked.

She thought about not answering, letting Chloe think she was asleep, but her friend had given her a place to retreat to. The least she could do was thank her for that. "Yeah."

The door opened slowly before Chloe poked her head through the opening. "Hey. How are you doing?"

Linnea took a shaky breath. "I've been better."

Chloe came fully into the room and sat on the

side of the bed. She took one of Linnea's hands between hers. "I'm so sorry. I want to do Michael bodily harm for hurting you, betraying you like that."

"You're not the only one."

"Did he give you any sort of explanation why he'd be that cruel?"

"I didn't give him the chance."

"Well, good. I can't imagine a single thing he could say that would make him any less of a worthless human being."

Linnea knew everything Chloe was saying was true, but it still hurt. She didn't want Michael to be a worthless human being. She wanted the past twenty-four hours to be nothing more than a horrible nightmare brought on by bad seafood. She desperately wanted to wake up from that nightmare to find that Michael was the loving, caring man he'd been over the past six months. But as she looked at the righteous anger in her best friend's eyes, she knew every horrible moment had been all too real.

Chloe squeezed Linnea's hand in what felt like a grip of solidarity. "I'm going to make you some French toast. It's never failed us before."

True, French toast had become their go-to breakfast whenever anything went wrong in college—bad grade, rotten date, even breakups. But this was so far beyond even the awesome healing properties of French toast.

"Don't you need to get to work?"

"I can go in later."

Linnea shook her head. "I don't want you shifting your life around for me."

"Don't be silly. You're my best friend. This is what best friends are for."

Linnea placed her free hand atop Chloe's. "Please don't take this the wrong way, but I don't think anything is going to help how I feel right now other than time. Or possibly a lobotomy."

The helpless look on Chloe's face nearly made Linnea cry again. But, bless her, Chloe nodded before she leaned forward and wrapped Linnea in her arms. Linnea had to bite her lip to keep tears from falling.

"You need anything, no matter how small or how big, you let me know. I know you like to be alone to deal with things, but sometimes it doesn't feel right, like now. It feels like I'm abandoning you."

Linnea pulled away. "You've given me the one thing I need most, a place to get away." *A place to hide*, a voice in her mind said. "Though I do feel bad about being in the way of your dad and brothers."

"Don't worry about that. And you know they've always liked you."

"Did you tell them what happened?"

Chloe shook her head. "No. That's not my place. Though Dad knew the wedding was off when I talked to him last night."

Linnea nodded. "I told Owen since I showed up out of the blue. Sorry I didn't call you back and let you know I was coming. I wasn't thinking."

"No need to apologize. You're here now, and you can stay however long you want to."

"Thanks." She glanced toward the sun streaming in the window, the cheery brightness so at odds with her mood. The downpour the night before had been a more suitable match.

Chloe stood, drawing Linnea's attention away from the window. "I'll go and get out of your hair. Make yourself at home, okay?"

Linnea nodded. When she heard the front door close, she tried to force herself from the bed. But in the end, she slid back under the covers and sank into her heartache again. In that moment, she hated Michael every bit as much as she'd ever loved him. This time, her tears were born of anger that he'd made her feel this way, that he'd stolen her will to even get out of bed and face the day.

When she woke again, the morning was about to give way to afternoon. She ached even worse than she had earlier that morning, and that, more than anything else, prompted her to finally get up. She walked to the window and looked out over the gentle rise and fall of the ranch that spread for miles. It was so different from where she'd grown up and now lived in Dallas, but she'd always liked it. She'd never met anyone who fit their surroundings more than the Brodys. It was as if the land were a member of their family, their flesh and blood. The closest she'd ever come to that kind of connection with a place was her shop, but when she thought of it now it felt as if that relationship had been stabbed in the heart, as well.

Linnea forced herself to pull some clean clothes from her bag and head to the bathroom. A shower wasn't going to heal her wounded heart, but maybe it would make her feel half-way human again.

She stood under the steaming stream of water, soaking the heat into her aching body, trying to forget why she felt so wretched. But the more she tried to forget that she'd nearly married an already married man, the more that horrible truth burned itself into her thoughts. By the time she got dressed and left the bathroom, she felt as if she'd worked an entire day. Who knew having your heart stomped on could be so exhausting?

When she reached the kitchen, it was past lunchtime. But she still nabbed a chocolate glazed donut from a bakery box. As she took the first bite, she noticed a note with her name on it sitting in the middle of the table.

Gone to get your tires fixed. Back later. O.

She smiled a little bit. Underneath the party boy exterior, Owen Brody just might have a nice streak in him.

She walked slowly through the house, pausing to look at familiar family photos. She was even in a couple of the snapshots with Chloe from their college days. They looked so happy and carefree. Hard to believe that little more than a day ago, she'd still been happy. But that emotion seemed so far away now.

Shaking her head at the self-pity that was threatening to consume her whole, she headed out onto the porch and the heat of the day. She stopped short when she saw her car parked in the graveled area between the house and the barn. Part of her sorrow gave way to guilt. While she was sleeping the morning away, Owen had already gotten her tires fixed and brought her car back to the ranch. She scanned the area but didn't see him. No doubt he was already out riding on the back forty somewhere, doing whatever ranchers did every day.

Despite still feeling shaky, she descended the steps and started walking. The day was quite warm, but she didn't care. Though she spent most of her time indoors working, there was something therapeutic about getting out in the sunshine under a wide blue sky. It almost made her believe things weren't so bad.

But they were.

She walked the length of the driveway and back. When she approached the house, Roscoe and Cletus, the Brodys' two lovable basset hounds, came ambling around the corner of the porch.

"Hey, guys," she said as she sank onto the front steps and proceeded to scratch them both under their chins. "You're just as handsome as ever."

"Why, thank you."

She jumped at the sound of Owen's voice. The dogs jumped, too, probably because she had. She glanced up to where Owen stood at the corner of the porch. "You made me scare the dogs."

"Sorry. But I was taught to thank someone when they pay me a compliment."

She shook her head. "Nice to see your ego is still intact."

"Ouch."

She laughed a little at his mock affront, something she wouldn't have thought possible that morning. She ought to thank him for that moment of reprieve, but she didn't want to focus on why she'd thought she might never laugh or even smile again. Instead, she nodded toward her car. "Thanks for getting the tires fixed so quickly. How much do I owe you?"

"Nothing."

"I'm perfectly capable of paying my own bills."

"I'm sure you are. Still, I don't think fixing a couple of flats is going to send me to the poorhouse." With that he tapped the brim of his cowboy hat and headed toward the barn.

As he walked away, she noticed how nice

he looked in those worn jeans. No wonder he didn't have trouble finding women.

Oh, my God! She was looking at Owen's butt. Owen, as in Chloe's little brother Owen. The kid who'd once waited on her and Chloe outside Chloe's room and doused them with a super-soaker, the guy who had earned the nickname Horndog Brody.

She jerked her gaze away, suddenly wondering if she was mentally deficient. First she nearly married a guy who was already married. And now, little more than a day after she found out she'd nearly become an unwitting bigamist, she was ogling her best friend's brother's ass.

Unsettled, she went back inside, but instantly felt at a loss for what to do. She was normally hawking wedding gowns, veils and tiaras, everything to make a bride feel like a princess on her special day. Now the idea of even stepping foot into her store made her stomach turn. She knew she'd have to find a way to get past that. She had too much invested in the shop, and she couldn't leave Katrina in the lurch for too long.

Her heart stuttered when she realized her own fairy-tale gown still hung in the back of the shop. After weeks of admiring it every day, she knew she never wanted to see it again. She grabbed her phone and called Katrina.

"Hey, sweetie," Katrina answered. "How are you doing?"

It was a miracle Linnea had remembered to even call Katrina the day before to let her know she was going out of town for a few days. In fact, she'd been an hour out of Dallas before it dawned on her.

"I'm out of bed, which is more than I thought I'd accomplish today. How are things going there?"

"Fine. Don't worry about the shop, okay?"

"Listen, I need you to do something for me."

"Name it."

"Sell my dress."

"What?"

"My dress. I don't want it to be there when I get back. Mark it at a price that moves it fast."

Katrina hesitated before responding, "Are you sure? You love that dress."

"I loved Michael, too, and look what that got me." She realized how sharp her response had been as soon as it left her mouth. "I'm sorry. It's just that it's a reminder of what a fool I am."

"You're not a fool. I was standing on the outside and didn't see any red flags, either."

Linnea knew that should make her feel better, but it didn't. "Has he called there looking for me?"

"A few times, but don't worry about that. I took care of it."

Something about the tone of Katrina's voice sounded as though more was going on. "What do you mean, you took care of it?"

"Well, he came by, demanding to know where

you were. I may have told him to leave, and if he came back I was going to call the cops and report him for stalking."

Linnea's mouth dropped open. "You didn't?"

"I did, and I'd do it again. I might be small, but I will mess up anyone who hurts my friends."

Despite everything, Linnea smiled. "Have I told you lately that you're awesome?"

"No, and you should do that more often."

"You're right. I'll make a note of that."

Katrina laughed, and it lifted Linnea's spirits some. They plummeted, however, when after she ended the call, she pulled up all the pre-wedding photos stored in her phone and started deleting them. With each one, it felt more and more as though the past six months of her life had been a waste. Despite what she'd told Katrina, she paused on the main photo of her gorgeous wedding gown. Yes, it was just a dress, but it had embodied her happiness, all her hopes and dreams for the future. Michael had robbed her of all that with his lies.

She hesitated with her finger over the last photo of the dress. As soon as she hit the Delete button, everything she'd planned for with such excitement would be well and truly gone. Fresh tears overflowed and ran down her cheeks as she hit the button.

Chapter Three

Owen was still in a foul mood when he reached the house. He was covered in mud literally from head to toe, thanks to a calf that had given him the slip. And because Linnea was visiting, he was going to have to wear the mud all the way through the house, probably dropping globs from the back door to the bathroom.

He took his boots off outside the back door and stepped into the house. As he passed from the mudroom into the kitchen, he nearly collided with Linnea. He reached out on instinct but managed to catch himself before he actually touched her.

Linnea took a step back and eyed him. "What on earth?"

"Another glamorous day in the life of a rancher." As if to punctuate his words, a blob of mud dropped off his arm onto the floor.

She motioned him back into the appropriately named mudroom. "Take off those clothes, and I'll put them in the wash."

He lifted an eyebrow. "Trying to get me out of my clothes?"

She rolled her eyes, and that's when he saw that her eyes were red as though she'd been crying again. He didn't know what had happened, but he didn't like seeing her so upset. He dated around, yeah, but he tried not to make any woman cry.

"Don't be such a twit," she said as she ushered him out of the kitchen. "Just dump those muddy things in there, and then I'll turn my back as you head through the house."

He turned around and retraced his steps.

"Getting bossed around by a woman. It's like Chloe never left."

"I suppose if I wasn't here, you'd just track mud through the house like an animal."

He unzipped his jeans and shoved them down his legs. "No, I'd strip like I'm doing now and walk through the house stark naked."

"Oh."

He laughed a little at her startled reaction. When he was down to his boxers, he headed for the kitchen. "Hide your eyes."

"The coast is clear."

When he stepped into the kitchen, he smiled at how rigidly she stood with her back to him. "No peeking."

"Don't worry. I don't want to burn my corneas."

"I'm that hot, huh?"

"Oh, good grief. Will you just get out of here?"

This time, he chuckled where she could hear him before heading to the bathroom.

LINNEA DIDN'T DARE turn around until she heard the water in the shower start running. She relaxed and headed for the mudroom, wondering why Owen's teasing had unnerved her so much. He'd always been a flirt, but he and Garrett had been more like brothers to her than anything else. They were actually the closest thing she'd ever had to brothers. But when she'd listened as he dropped his filthy clothes on the floor and walked into the kitchen behind her, she'd had to fight the urge to peek.

She shook her head, chalking it up to how mixed up she'd felt since Danielle Benson dropped her information bomb right in the middle of Linnea's life.

When she picked up the dirty jeans and shirt, they felt as if they had ten pounds of mud caked onto them. What did he do, mud-wrestle a cow?

She added the once white socks to the pile and was strangely grateful not to find a pair of underwear. At least she hadn't been standing in the same room with her best friend's buck-naked brother.

Unless he went commando.

Oh, good grief, why had that image popped into her head? She didn't need to think about whether or not Owen Brody wore underwear every time she looked at him.

She took the clothes into the laundry room and washed some of the mud out in the utility sink, thinking the whole time that perhaps she needed to shove her head under the cold stream of water, too.

She waited until she heard the shower turn off before starting the washing machine, then returned to the kitchen. A few minutes later, Owen walked back into the kitchen, this time clean and fully clothed. His dark hair was still wet, and something about that look caused a funny little flutter inside her.

She turned her gaze back to the countertop in front of her, wishing she could speed time up until she felt normal again, when her heart didn't feel as if it'd been stomped and when she wasn't having strange thoughts about Owen, whom she'd known since he was fourteen. Granted, he was twice that now, had grown into a man's body, but she still shouldn't even notice things like that. Especially when she'd been about to marry another man she'd loved very much. Probably part of her did still love Michael even if she hated him, too. You weren't supposed to be able to just turn love off and on like a light switch, right?

She mentally shook her head. This was probably just some sort of coping mechanism, her subconscious trying to find someone to make her feel good in the aftermath of being so horribly wronged by the man who had claimed he loved her.

"What are you doing?" Owen's voice pulled her from her rambling self-diagnosis.

"Cooking dinner."

"You don't have to do that. The chili wasn't that bad, was it?"

"No, it was fine. I just…needed something to do."

Owen leaned a hip against the opposite end of the counter. "You okay?"

He sounded hesitant, as though he wasn't used to asking people about their feelings. He was a guy. Of course he wasn't making a habit of in-depth conversations about feelings.

"Fine. Just wanted something to occupy my mind." She was saved from having to explain any further when Garrett walked in.

"It smells great in here. Hasn't smelled this good since Chloe left."

Linnea shifted her gaze to Owen and Chloe's

big brother. "I doubt that. I had a bowl of the chili. It was actually quite tasty."

"Why, thank you," Owen said, drawing her gaze back to him.

"You made the chili?"

He crossed his arms over his chest. "Don't sound so surprised. I'm good at more than riding a horse."

"That's not what I hear from the girls you've dated," Garrett said.

Owen slugged his brother in the arm. "Since when do you even talk to girls? You have longer conversations with the cattle."

Linnea managed to smile at the same brotherly poking at each other that she'd witnessed from the moment she'd met Chloe's family. It was a small comfort that some things didn't change. But then, some things did.

She tore her gaze away, ostensibly to refocus on the food preparation. But it was really to blink new tears into submission. She was so sick of crying, of how it made her feel even worse. She wanted to be the person again who could laugh at Owen and Garrett's antics, who could move through her day without feeling as though her emotions were riding a seesaw.

When she heard Chloe and Wyatt arrive, followed shortly thereafter by Chloe's dad, she forcibly shoved away her sadness. There was time enough later for it to leak out when she was alone.

Chloe came over and gave her a one-armed hug. "You shouldn't have done this," she said so no one else could hear her.

"I needed to. A gal can only cry so much before she feels like her head is going to pop off." Not that she didn't expect more tears to visit her later that night, or in the days ahead, no matter that she wanted to be done with them.

"Okay, then. What can I do to help?"

"Start pouring drinks."

A few minutes later, they all sat down to the

dinner she'd prepared, lasagna with salads and garlic bread.

"This is great, Lin," Chloe said.

"Yeah, way better than when Wyatt tried to cook for us when he was staying here," Owen added.

"Oh, the frozen chicken episode," Linnea said as she glanced across the table at Wyatt. "Heard all about that."

Wyatt shook his head. "Y'all are never going to let me live that down, are you?"

"Nope." Garrett's single-word answer set everyone to laughing.

Everyone but Linnea, although she managed a smile so it wasn't so obvious. She hadn't been lying when she said she'd cooked the meal to have something to do, and in appreciation for the Brodys letting her crash in their home for a few days. But as she saw the loving looks and small touches that passed between Chloe and Wyatt, Linnea would swear her heart was bleeding. She doubted anyone else even noticed those little evidences of a young couple in love, but she'd been no different only a couple of days before. It hurt to think about how all those adoring gazes and thrilling touches were gone forever.

The weight in her chest and the lump in her throat grew throughout the rest of dinner, to the point where she thought she might have to excuse herself. But somehow she managed to make it all the way through dessert. When she started to gather the dishes, Wayne stopped her.

"No, dear. You've done enough for tonight."

By the time Chloe and Wyatt left a few minutes later, Linnea felt as if a bear were sitting on her chest. She slipped out the front door while the guys cleaned up the kitchen. The night air was still warm as she stepped out under a wide, starry sky. But none of that offered her any comfort as she walked toward the fence near the barn.

She leaned her arms against the top rail and looked up at the sky in time to see a shooting star. Without even thinking, she made a wish for the pain inside her to go away, to maybe even someday be happy again.

A sob broke free and she laid her head atop her arms and cried yet again, as if her body could produce an endless supply of tears. Linnea didn't know how long she cried, but the worst was over when she heard a door close. She wiped the last of her tears from her cheeks, glad for the darkness should whoever had stepped outside come close.

She stared out across the darkened field as the sound of footsteps approached. Somehow she knew it was Owen before he came to stand beside her, propping his own arms on the fence.

"You overdosed on Brodys, didn't you?"

She laughed the merest bit at that. "How did you know?"

"Keen sense of observation. It's a gift."

She glanced his way and lifted an eyebrow. "Is there any talent you won't claim?"

"Ballet. Never got the hang of it."

She laughed for real this time, drawing a smile from Owen that lit an ember of warmth in her heart. "Thanks."

"For what?"

"For trying to make me feel better."

His gaze met hers. "How am I doing?"

She thought about it for a moment. "Okay." She'd like to say that all the pain was gone, but she knew that wasn't going away overnight, no matter how funny and nice Owen was to her. "I'm sorry if I'm a downer to be around now."

"You don't have anything to be sorry about. I just don't like to see you sad. It's so unlike you."

"I guess heartache catches up to all of us at some point."

"Yeah."

Something about the way Owen stared out

across the field, as if his thoughts were somewhere else, made her wonder what he was thinking about. Maybe he was remembering losing his mom when he was a child. She couldn't imagine how horrible that had been, even though she knew the story well of how his mother had been killed by a hit-and-run driver.

Linnea experienced the most unexpected sense of connection with him in that moment. She took a deep breath and stared out into the expanse of darkness as well. Her eyes had adjusted to the dim light enough that she could now pick out a few cows in the distance. She took a slow, deep breath.

"I still can't believe I almost married someone who is already married." She saw Owen shift toward her out of the corner of her eye.

"How did you find out?"

"His wife showed up at the shop. Surprise!"

"God, Linnea, I'm sorry. Who the hell does that?"

"Obviously the guy I thought I was going to spend the rest of my life with. Says a lot about my judgment, doesn't it?"

"Sounds to me more like he's a bastard in need of a good ass kicking."

"I thought about it, but that means I'd have to see his lying face again. Decided it wasn't worth it."

Owen was quiet for a while, but she could feel the anger coming off him. Oddly, it made her feel better.

"I know it sucks, but I'm glad you found out before you married him."

"Me, too." And she realized it was true. Though she was shredded inside, it would have been so much worse to find out the truth after she'd gone through with the wedding. What a nightmare that would have been.

They stood there, side by side, in silence for several minutes before Owen stepped away from the fence. "I'll stop invading your space."

"If anyone is invading anyone's space, it's me."

"Let that go. You know you might as well be part of the family."

"Thanks, again."

He nodded. "No problem. And if you decide Michael needs a good beat-down to make you feel better, just let me know. That can be arranged."

"He's not worth your time, either."

"I don't know. Might make me feel better."

She smiled at Owen. "I'm sure you can find something more fun to do."

He made a sound that seemed to say he wasn't sure about that, and though she truly didn't want him to go beat up Michael, she appreciated the thought.

After he said good-night, she faced the field again. It took a few minutes to realize it, but her heart felt lighter than it had when Owen came outside. She glanced back at the house. Even though she wasn't really hot on the male half of the species at the moment, she had to say the Brody men were the exceptions. Especially the youngest of them.

WHEN OWEN STEPPED INSIDE, he glanced back through the window to see that Linnea was still standing at the fence staring off into the night. He hoped she wasn't crying again, because the ass she'd been engaged to wasn't worth her tears.

"She okay?" Garrett asked as he walked into the living room from the kitchen.

Owen turned to face his brother. "Been crying."

"I heard her last night."

"Did Chloe tell you what happened?"

Garrett shook his head. "No. All I know is what you said, that the wedding had been called off."

"The jerk was already married."

Garrett's forehead wrinkled. "Lots of people have been married before. Did he not tell her?"

"No, he wasn't married before. He's still married. His wife showed up at Lin's shop and dropped the bomb."

Garrett cursed as Owen had when he heard the reason Linnea's wedding was off.

"Good thing he's nowhere near me right now." Owen might not be everyone's first pick as the most reliable, steady guy around, but you didn't mess with his family. And Linnea had become a part of the family the first time she spent a spring break at the ranch with Chloe. He'd defend her the same as he would his sister.

Even after he went to bed, he couldn't calm down enough to sleep. He hated that Linnea had shed one tear over Michael, that he'd given her cause for tears. No matter how much he thought about it, he couldn't figure out why someone would do what Michael had done. That was seriously messed up.

He fell asleep at some point after he heard Linnea come back inside, but when he woke up the next morning, the same pissed-off feeling was still clinging to him. He hated seeing injustices go unpunished, had ever since he was a little kid mourning the loss of his mother.

No, he didn't want to think about that, especially not in the mood he was in. Instead, he shoved the quilt off his legs and got out of bed, dressed and headed out to the barn before the sun was fully up for the day. He wanted to use the time to work with the horse he'd bought to train.

After he'd worked with the big gray for about half an hour, the pent-up anger eased. He'd still likely punch Michael if he ever saw him, but working with the horse had soothed the savage beast a bit.

"Time to get to work," his dad said as he and Garrett walked past the corral toward the barn.

Owen stopped and stared at their retreating

backs, wondering what the hell his dad thought he was doing. Killing time? It was no use trying to explain that he was working, though. And a part of him understood why his dad and brother didn't think his interest in training horses would last. After all, he hadn't stuck with anything else over the years.

But this was different. All the rest he'd done because he was bored, wanting to try something different, unable to settle. But from the moment he'd realized he was more interested in what it took to make a good rodeo horse than actually riding in rodeo events, it was as if a fire had started within him. As if horse training might actually be his thing, his way to make his own mark on the family legacy. Garrett, as the oldest, was his father's protégé on the ranch and seemed to be cut from the same cloth as their dad. Chloe's domain had ventured into medicine even though she still pitched in plenty around the ranch when she could. Owen was ready to be known for something other than the family party boy. He just had to prove to his family that he was serious about it.

Until he could do that, he saddled up for another day tending to the cattle herd and checking fencing. As he rode out of the barn, he noticed Linnea sitting on the porch with a cup of coffee. She waved when she saw him, and he smiled as he tapped the brim of his hat with his index finger. He hadn't heard her cry herself to sleep the night before, and that made him happy. An odd sense of pride filled him that maybe he'd had a small part to do with that. He just hoped that another day of hanging around the house alone didn't give her too much time to fall back into that pit of sadness she'd been in. She needed to stay busy, and the perfect idea for how to help her stay out of her funk popped into his head. His smile grew as he followed his dad and brother out through the pasture for another day of work.

As LINNEA HUNG UP on the last phone call she needed to make to completely cancel her wedding, she didn't know whether to feel relieved or empty. She did know that she should go back to Dallas, return to her life and her business. She'd been hiding out at the Brodys' ranch for the better part of a week, and she suspected they'd like to have their man cave back.

But the idea of getting in her car and leaving the nice little cocoon the ranch provided made her stomach tie in knots. What if despite Katrina's threat, Michael showed up at the shop the moment Linnea got back? She wanted to be strong enough to believe that it wouldn't bother her, but she doubted she would be. She'd bought into their romance a hundred percent, and she still sometimes thought she might wake up to find the awful truth wasn't in fact the truth.

She needed to stop thinking that way and face it head-on, no matter how horrible it was going to be. She knew that, told herself that over and over, and yet here she sat in Chloe's old room, not taking that first step.

A knock on the door drew her attention. "Yeah?"

Owen poked his head in. "Get dressed. We're going to the rodeo."

"I don't think I'm up for that, but you all have a good time."

"Nope, not letting you wiggle your way out of this one. After all, you're my only hope."

She cocked her head a little to the side. "Do I even want to ask?"

"See, there's this girl named Tiffany in town who has been after me, and I need protection."

Linnea actually snorted at that. "Protection from a woman? You are Owen Brody, right?"

"Exactly. I'm so irresistible that I need a protection detail."

"Lord, I need to borrow some waders because it is getting deep in here."

Owen shot her one of those crooked grins

of his that she was sure had the women of Blue Falls tripping over themselves to be with him. For a moment, she understood why. If he weren't Chloe's brother and she didn't think men sucked at the moment, she might even be tempted.

Which was another good reason not to go to the rodeo, and another reason she needed to get back to Dallas.

"Owen—"

"You're going to leave me out to dry after I saved you from a rainstorm and got your tires fixed?"

"Pulling out all the stops, huh?"

"Did it work?"

"Why are you pushing this? Do you really need me to pretend I'm with you to stave off the hordes of women?"

He leaned back against the doorframe and hung his thumbs in his jean pockets. "Because you need to get out of this house and have a good time."

"You do remember I just had the worst week of my life, right?"

"Which is why you need to go have some fun, because I'd lay good money down that Michael isn't having fun right now."

The evil gleam in Owen's eyes nearly made her laugh. It was amazing how many times he'd given her a light moment throughout the week, something she would have thought impossible when she'd driven out of Dallas with her world shattered.

"Fine, I'll go. But I'm not promising you won't regret it later."

"Fair enough, but you'll be with me. You're guaranteed to have a good time."

"Oh, get out," she said as she stood. "And take your enormous ego with you."

His grin widened as he slipped out the door. She closed it behind him and shook her head.

But she found herself smiling at the idea of spending the night out while Michael was miserable. At least she hoped he was.

She turned and headed for her bag to look for something appropriate to wear. She might not really be Owen Brody's date, but damn if she wasn't going to take advantage of his infectious thirst for a good time. And if she happened to appreciate how he looked in his jeans, well, nobody had to know but her. After all, she'd be back home soon, back to her real life that didn't include rodeos or cowboys in tight jeans. She glanced toward the door where Owen had stood a few moments before and wondered if she would have been better off falling for someone like him than for the man she'd thought was perfect for her.

Chapter Four

Despite the fact that her best friend had lived her entire life on a ranch and had probably been going to rodeos since she was in utero, Linnea found herself asking several questions as she and the Brodys sat in the grandstands watching the events.

Owen nudged her in the back. "I thought you grew up in Texas, woman."

She eyed him over her shoulder. "Not too many rodeos in the Dallas suburbs."

"Not that far to Fort Worth, either. Home to one of the biggest rodeos in the country."

"She was probably watching *Project Runway*

or *Say Yes to the Dress*," Chloe said with a teasing smile.

Linnea wrinkled her nose at her friend. "Neither of those was on when I was in high school. And I seem to remember someone I know not minding *Project Runway* marathons."

Chloe lifted an eyebrow. "I am a girl, after all. Just because I know my way around horses and cattle doesn't mean I don't like pretty things, too."

Linnea noticed Owen turn his attention to his brother beside him. "How did talking about rodeo lead to a discussion about clothes?"

"Get two women together, and talk always turns toward clothes," Garrett said with a matter-of-fact tone. "Or shoes."

Chloe reached back and slugged him in the side of the leg.

"Ow. Wyatt, control your wife."

"Oh, hell no," Wyatt said, putting his hands

in the air. "Not touching that one with a ten-foot pole."

"Smart boy," Wayne said from where he sat on the other side of Garrett.

"What is up with women needing so many shoes?" Owen asked.

"Because we have pretty feet," Chloe said.

"I'll have you know I have gorgeous feet," he tossed back.

"Boy, the only time you had anything other than ugly feet was when you were born."

Linnea found herself smiling at the good-natured family teasing. Owen had been right. It felt good to get out of the house and do something around other people, even if every time she saw a couple holding hands it sent a sharp pain through her heart.

By the time the rodeo was over, she was ready to retreat to the guest room, however. She was proud of herself for taking a step toward moving on, but she'd worn a smile for about as long as she could manage for one night.

So when Owen pulled into the parking lot for the Blue Falls Music Hall, a flutter of panic hit her. "I thought we were heading back to the house."

"Later."

Before she could protest, he slipped out of the truck and headed around the front. Not willing to let him get the door for her as if it were a date, she opened her own door and got out before he could reach her. Thankfully, he didn't comment on her blocking his attempt at chivalry.

"Sure you don't want to skip this?" she asked.

"You haven't been to the music hall in a long time. And the Teagues of Texas, a local band, is playing tonight. They're pretty good considering it's not what they do for a living."

Not wanting to put a damper on Owen's fun, she accompanied him inside. Though she wasn't his date, it was obvious that they'd arrived together. But it didn't seem to matter. They were approximately half a dozen steps inside when a cute little brunette grabbed his hand and dragged him toward the dance floor. He looked back at Linnea with a smile and a shrug, causing her to laugh a little under her breath.

"Oh, good, you came," Chloe said as she looped her arm with Linnea's and dragged her toward the bar.

"Not much of a choice. Seems all my options for a ride back to the ranch stopped here." She could have driven herself, should have, but it had seemed silly to take yet another vehicle at the time when they were all going to and coming back to the same place. But now she was stuck in the middle of a beehive of humanity having a good time.

After they sat at the bar and ordered drinks,

Chloe spun toward Linnea. "How are you doing?"

"Great. Never better."

"Sorry. We were hoping getting out would give you a boost."

She took a breath. "It did." When Chloe looked skeptical, Linnea continued. "Really."

Even if she was feeling as if her meager reserve of happiness was running out like the sand rushing through an hourglass, she needed to be grateful that she had friends so ready to try to help her. But maybe it was time to go home and continue trying to heal there.

But she thought about how differently her family would handle things. While they were wonderful and loving, too, she knew her mother would want to hug and protect her, to talk about all the minute details of what had happened. The very thought made Linnea want to run screaming across the border into Mexico. Even though she would have preferred going back to the ranch after the rodeo, being in the midst of a crowd of strangers dancing, talking and laughing was still better than the pity and well-intended coddling she would get from her family if she went home. She needed more time to prepare to deal with that every bit as much as for dealing with returning to work and possibly running into Michael.

She scanned the crowd, spotting a few familiar faces. Chloe's friends India and Skyler were laughing in the opposite corner with someone else Linnea didn't know. Garrett and Wyatt were standing at the end of the bar holding bottles of beer. But, no surprise, Owen was right in the middle of the action on the dance floor, smiling at the girl he was dancing with, not the same one who'd accosted him at the door. Linnea realized she'd been staring at him for too long, appreciating the way he moved and how nice he looked in a clean, dark blue, button-up shirt and jeans that weren't caked with a day's work.

"Did you hear me?"

Linnea jerked her attention back to Chloe. "What?"

Chloe looked toward the dance floor. "What were you watching so intently?"

"Nothing. Just got lost in my thoughts." Let Chloe assume she was still dwelling on what Michael had done. It was better than admitting that she had been thinking about Chloe's little brother in a way she shouldn't be, especially only days before she had been scheduled to walk down the aisle to marry another man. What the heck was wrong with her?

Chloe didn't look as if she quite believed her, but she didn't question her further. She did look back at the dancers, however, and shook her head. "I swear, one of these days my brother is going to grow up and stop acting like a college frat boy."

"Holding your breath on that one?"

Chloe laughed. "No. Don't really want to turn blue and pass out."

Linnea chanced another glance at Owen. "It's not like he's over the hill." Far from it. He was a man in his prime, one she needed to stop watching before she gave herself away. There shouldn't even be anything to give away. Or maybe she was just overreacting because her nerves were so on edge.

"Would you like to dance?"

It took Linnea a moment to realize she was the one a tall cowboy was talking to. He was nice-looking in a rough-around-the-edges sort of way. He just had the misfortune of asking her to dance at the wrong time in her life.

"No, but thank you."

"You sure?"

She offered him a smile that she hoped was kind but not encouraging. "Yes, I am."

The song ended, and Owen parted from his

latest dance partner. As if he could sense they were talking about him, he headed straight for them. He eyed the retreating cowboy.

"That guy bothering you?" he asked.

Linnea shook her head. "No. Just asked me to dance."

The band struck up another tune, a cover of a Jason Aldean song. Linnea was more of a pop-music fan, but you couldn't live in Texas and not be familiar on some level with country music.

"Not a bad idea," Owen said, and extended his hand to her.

She stared at his hand for a moment. "I don't think so."

He placed his other hand over his heart. "You're going to shoot me down? The guy who saved you from the side of the road."

"Oh, you're milking that for all it's worth."

"Go on," Chloe said, motioning toward the

dance floor. "Save my brother from his legions of adoring fangirls."

Linnea had the strongest urge to click her heels together three times to see if she'd be transported back to the ranch. Something tightened inside her, telling her that dancing with Owen wasn't a good idea. Mentally calling herself a fool for worrying over nothing, she sighed. "Okay, one dance."

He gave her a crooked grin. "Unless you can't pull yourself away."

Linnea met Chloe's gaze. "You're right. He is an ego-driven frat boy."

"Hey," Owen said.

She just rolled her eyes at his mock offense and walked past him toward the dance floor. When he joined her there, however, taking one of her hands in his and placing his other at her waist, she tensed involuntarily.

Owen didn't seem to notice as he spun her

deeper into the crowd. "Are you having a good time?"

"Actually, yes. Thank you for urging me to get out tonight." She might still be hurting, but she also was able to recognize that moping around in the guest room at the ranch wasn't going to alleviate that pain.

"Good."

She looked up at Owen and momentarily got trapped by his gaze. While she'd spent plenty of time with Owen over the years, she'd never been this close to him outside of an occasional quick hug hello or goodbye. She'd never thought about him in a physical way, never wondered how it would feel to have his strong hand wrapped around hers, certainly never yearned to move closer to him. At that thought, her body tingled with an electric warmth that caused her step to falter. Owen's grip on her tightened as if to prevent her from falling.

"You okay?"

"Yeah. Just clumsy."

He smiled. "I get that a lot, women tripping over their own feet at the sight of me."

She laughed a little, and wondered if it sounded as forced to him as it did her own ears. Because he'd hit entirely too close to the truth, as in on the nose. A flutter of panic danced through her when she thought she saw a question in his eyes. Unwilling to answer it, at least not truthfully, she lowered her gaze and shifted all her focus to making the right dance moves.

Owen led her around the dance floor for the remainder of the song, but after it was over he didn't protest when she moved away and headed back to the bar. In fact, he seemed as if he couldn't wait to move on to his next dance partner. That shouldn't hurt, but it did. She told herself it was only because she was already wounded and her emotions were tender to even the simplest touch, the merest slight.

Chloe was dancing with Wyatt, so Linnea had

a few minutes to get herself together before she had to face her friend, the one who could typically see right through her. Though she should keep her gaze firmly planted on her drink, she turned so that she could see Owen dancing with a beautiful blonde who was laughing at something he'd said. A twinge of disappointment curled up in her chest. Why should she even care who he danced with? She shouldn't. And yet as she watched him pull the blonde closer, something twisted inside her.

"You ask me, you got away from that one just in time."

Linnea glanced left and realized the woman who'd stepped up to the bar was talking to her. "Pardon?"

The young woman, yet another blonde, gestured over her shoulder toward the dance floor with her thumb. "Owen Brody. You don't want to get messed up with that one. He goes through women faster than most men go through socks."

She turned her back to the bar and glanced toward the sea of dancers. "That man could make loving and leaving an Olympic sport, and he'd take the gold medal."

"We're just old friends," Linnea said, reminding herself as much as she was explaining to the other woman.

"Uh-huh. I wonder how many women here started out as just friends with Owen. Trust me. Leave it at that."

The woman took her drink and wandered off through the crowd, leaving Linnea feeling oddly irritated. What was she thinking, letting herself feel anything other than friendship for someone known for playing the field? Was she so desperate to be loved that she was latching onto the first guy to cross her path after Michael's betrayal?

She shook her head as if that would work to clear out the crazy thoughts she'd been having. Owen wasn't anything other than a friend. She was just letting her vulnerable state make her think weird things.

As another song ended, she focused on the lead singer of the band.

"We've had a special request tonight, and we just couldn't say no to this one." He motioned for someone to come up to the stage. When a young man she recognized as one of the steer wrestlers from the rodeo hopped up on the stage, the singer continued. "Jacob here has a question he wants to ask someone special."

As Jacob stepped to the microphone, Linnea's heart started beating faster. No, this couldn't be what she thought it was. Not tonight, of all nights.

Jacob looked nervous as he smiled. "A year ago, I met someone right here after a rodeo. We had our first dance here, and I think I fell in love with her that night."

A murmur of appreciation went through the crowd, but Linnea felt as if the world were caving in on her. As though she were watching a train wreck happen in slow motion, she couldn't force herself to look away let alone get out of the building.

The young cowboy pulled a ring from his pocket and extended it. "Chelsea Billings, will you marry me?"

Dizziness slammed into Linnea with such force that she had to grab the edge of the bar to keep from tipping over. Air, she needed air. She somehow stayed on her feet as she pushed her way through the cheering crowd toward the door. By the time she stumbled outside, she felt as if her lungs had shrunk to the size of lima beans. Memories assailed her as she made her way through the rows of vehicles to Owen's truck. She gripped the side of the bed and sucked in deep gulps of air.

She didn't want to let Michael ruin her belief in good people, in the idea that true love was possible, but he'd certainly damaged them. As she'd watched that young cowboy propose, she couldn't help wondering if he had some secret life, if the words coming out of his mouth were lies.

The moment tears pooled in her eyes, anger welled in her. The need to scream nearly consumed her. Instead, she slapped the side of the truck, imagining it was Michael and his lies. As she let some of the anger out, she hit the truck again, and again. She didn't know if she could ever stop.

OWEN WAS ABOUT to get the phone number of his latest dancing partner when he felt a peck on his shoulder. He turned to find his sister looking up at him.

"Have you seen Linnea?" Chloe asked.

He scanned the crowd. "Last I saw her, she was headed for the bar."

"I can't find her anywhere."

"Maybe she went to the bathroom."

"Nope. I looked."

"Well, unless she hitchhiked back to the ranch, she's got to be here somewhere." There had been something he couldn't identify in her eyes earlier, but he'd chalked it up to her being tired, or perhaps not in a party mood. It certainly couldn't have been what his first impression had told him, that she'd been seeing him as something more than her best friend's brother. They'd known each other too long, hung out too many times, and women who'd just been through what she had didn't get over it that quickly.

As Chloe moved away to look for Linnea in another corner of the building, his gaze settled on the newly engaged couple.

"Damn it," he said. That's why they couldn't find Linnea. Probably the last thing she'd wanted to watch was a couple starting toward their happily ever after when hers had been blown to bits around her.

He glanced back to where he'd left his dancing partner standing to find she'd already found another guy to pay attention to her. Fine by Owen. He made for the exit, figuring that if Linnea was nowhere to be found inside, logic had to point the way outside.

She wasn't immediately visible when he stepped out the door, but he heard her before he saw her. By the way she was smacking her hand against the side of his truck, she was definitely upset. A strange knot formed in his stomach as he hoped he wasn't part of the reason for her meltdown.

He approached her slowly, trying to figure out how to handle the situation. He'd never been good with women who were upset and usually made himself scarce. But she looked so alone, so in pain that he couldn't do that.

"Lin?"

She spun toward him, and the tears streaking

down her face made him ache for her and get angry all at the same time.

He took another step toward her. "He's not worth you tearing yourself up like this."

"I know that." She turned to face the side of the truck again, gripping the edge of the metal with such force that he wondered if she was imagining it was Michael's neck. "I want all this rage and pain to go away, but…it sometimes feels like it's getting worse instead of better." Her voice broke, and she sniffed against a fresh wave of tears. "I don't understand what I did to deserve this."

Those words carved straight through his heart. How many times had he wondered the same thing?

Owen closed the distance between them and pulled her into his arms. He knew nothing he said would make her feel better, but he had to try something. Suffering alone was the worst feeling a person could have. He knew that from experience. "You didn't do anything to deserve what that bastard did to you. He's just a pitiful excuse for a human being."

He could tell she was trying to hold her tears inside, but the pain wouldn't be contained. Her stiff posture relaxed some as she leaned against his chest and cried. Without thinking, he lifted his hand and smoothed her long red hair and cradled her closer. If she needed to cry all night to get that piece of garbage out of her system, he'd let her. Because what Linnea needed now more than anything was a friend, one around whom she didn't have to pretend she was okay.

He knew Chloe would do anything in the world for Linnea, but he'd also seen the look on Linnea's face when she watched Chloe with Wyatt. It was one part yearning, one part sadness, but another part happiness for the newlyweds. He didn't have to hear Linnea's thoughts to know she didn't want to do anything to dampen their joy of starting a life together.

They stood there in the parking lot for a long time, but eventually Linnea's sobs grew quiet. When she finally pulled away, he didn't release her. Despite her obvious sorrow, he realized he hadn't minded holding her close. It had felt good to offer her comfort, better still that she'd accepted it and let him gather her to him. When she looked up, it hit him how pretty she was even with tearstained cheeks.

Oh, hell no. He couldn't think of Linnea in that way, not with his track record. Especially not when she was still hurting over Michael. He reminded himself that Linnea needed a friend, not another guy trying to make a move on her when she was vulnerable.

But what had been that look she'd given him when they'd been dancing? He'd seen enough women look at him with interest to know it when he saw it.

No, he was wrong. Even if she had seen him that way for a moment, it was because her emotions were all messed up. She was feeling un-loved and unwanted, and she was confusing his kindness for something else. And then he'd come out here and held her in his arms.

He told himself to step away, to break con-tact, but he found himself fighting the urge to let his fingers drift across her cheeks to wipe away her tears, to see if her skin was as soft as it looked in the faint light. Before he lost his grip on his willpower, he released her arms and took a couple of steps back from her.

"I don't know about you, but I'm done in for the night," he said.

She looked at him with a questioning expres-sion for a moment before she nodded. "Yeah, I'm pretty tired. Making a fool of yourself can do that."

"You didn't make a fool of yourself. Some-times life just sucks and you have to punch a truck."

The faint smile that tugged at her lips elicited

a smile from him, as well. And a strange, tingling warmth sprang to life in his chest. He'd made lots of women smile in his life, but there was something about helping Linnea smile even the faintest bit in the midst of her pain that put all those other smiles to shame. Before he could do something stupid like let those thoughts tumble out of his mouth, he opened his truck door and motioned for Linnea to climb in.

Quiet settled between them as he drove them back to the ranch. When he parked in his usual spot between the house and barn a few minutes later, he cut the engine and reached for his door.

"Owen."

The sound of his name and the feel of Linnea's small hand grasping his stopped him. When he glanced across the cab at her, Lin looked uncharacteristically shy. But there was a shine in her eyes that had him squeezing her hand and enjoying the contact more than he should.

"Thank you for letting me blubber all over you back there."

"Eh, this shirt was ready for the laundry anyway."

She smiled again, a little more than earlier. "I mean it. I keep thinking that I can't possibly cry any more over this whole mess, and then I go and do it again."

"Maybe tonight was the last time."

"I hope so. You were right when you said he's not worth my tears."

"You deserve someone who is honest and will treat you right."

"Like Wyatt does for Chloe?"

"Yeah. Of course, he knows if he doesn't, he has to answer to my dad, Garrett and me." He ran his thumb across the top of her hand, surprising himself and, judging by her expression, Linnea, as well. "We'd do the same for you in a heartbeat, you know that."

She broke eye contact and nodded. "I do, and

I appreciate it. But you all have already done enough by giving me a place to go while I get my head on straight, and by getting me out away from my moping. I need to deal with the rest on my own."

He'd halfway hoped she'd changed her mind so he could go give Michael Benson the lesson he deserved. Owen wasn't normally violent, but just the thought of what Michael had done to Lin made him want to go caveman all over the bastard.

The silence that followed grew a little awkward, and Owen knew he should release Linnea's hand. The fact that he didn't want to was what finally forced him to let go.

Chapter Five

The next morning, though Linnea was awake when she heard the Brody men begin to stir, she stayed in her room. The moment her eyes had opened to a new day, everything that had happened the night before came rushing back. Not only had she bawled like a baby all over Owen's shirt, but she was afraid her odd feelings toward him had shown when she met his eyes on the dance floor, and maybe again in the truck when they returned to the ranch.

The fact that he'd held her hand, even caressed it, didn't do anything to clarify the situation. If anything, it made her even more confused.

How was it possible to feel an attraction toward someone else so soon after the break with Michael, the man she'd been about to marry? And the fact that she'd known Owen for years with no similar feelings just made her feel even more as though she was losing her mind.

She waited until she heard the horses ride out for another day of work on the ranch before she left the bedroom and got ready for... whatever she was going to do to fill her day. She needed to return to Dallas, but that little voice of doubt kept whispering that she wasn't ready to face that just yet. The ranch was so peaceful, and she knew that life would turn back into a whirlwind if she went home. She'd have to face her family and their questions and looks of concern.

After eating a donut, she wandered out to the front porch. She bent to scratch Roscoe and Cletus between their ears, then descended the porch steps and headed toward the barn.

Though the horses scared her a little, she liked visiting with them when they were safely on the other side of their stall doors.

She made the turn into the barn and slammed right into Owen. He reached for her with one hand, but when the horse he'd been leading out reared, he had to focus all his attention on the animal. Off balance, Linnea tripped and fell backward onto her butt. But the surprise of falling was eclipsed by the sight of the horse's hooves pawing the air above her.

"Whoa, girl," Owen said as he urged the horse back down onto all fours and backed the mare farther into the barn. He glanced at Linnea as he soothed the horse. "You okay?"

"Yeah." She stood and dusted off the back of her jeans. "Sorry about slamming into you."

He smiled. "I was about to say the same thing."

The horse sidestepped, and Linnea instinctively backed away.

"She won't hurt you," Owen said.

"I'm not so sure about that."

He motioned Linnea toward him. "Come on. Give her a little rub, and she'll be your friend for life."

"I think it's better if there's a good bit of real estate between us."

His eyebrows drew together. "Are you afraid of horses?"

She shrugged. "Maybe."

"But you've ridden, right? I'm sure Chloe's had you out here before."

"I've been on a horse exactly once, and let's just say that it didn't end well. And it wasn't here."

He shook his head. "You're a Texan. How can you not ride?"

She propped her hands against her hips. "Because there's not exactly a lot of call for horseback riding in the streets of Dallas."

"I could teach you."

"I'm fine with both feet on the ground, thanks."

He shot her a crooked grin. "Chicken."

"Yep. Bwak, bwak."

Owen laughed, and the sound caused a really unwise fluttering in her chest.

"So, you headed off to meet your dad and brother?"

"No, not until this afternoon. I've got a rare morning to do my own work." He led the horse out of the barn, causing Linnea to back up even more.

She didn't relax until he had the horse in the large corral next to the barn. With a fence between her and the powerful animal, she moved closer and noticed the three barrels spaced out in a triangular formation. "You rejoining the rodeo circuit as a barrel racer?"

He glanced at her. "Not quite. I'm training her to be a barrel-racing horse and hope to sell her."

Linnea laid her arms along the top slat of the fence. "How long have you been doing that?"

"A few months. Charlotte here is my first attempt." He swung up into the saddle and rode Charlotte to a spot that would approximate a starting spot for barrel racing, then kicked the mare's sides.

Charlotte sped toward the first barrel, and she was a beauty in motion. But Linnea's eyes went to Owen, the way his long legs gripped the horse's sides, the easy way he leaned into the turns. He was every inch the cowboy, as at home with the horse as she had always been with dresses and shoes. While he had a boatload of sex appeal, just watching him in his natural habitat told her all she needed to know about her ill-advised attraction. Even if she wasn't coming off the worst breakup imaginable, she and Owen had about as much in common as a pair of worn cowboy boots did with Manolo Blahnik pumps.

Even so, she couldn't take her eyes off him. The part of her that wanted to feel alive and attractive started imagining what it would be like to be with him, even for only a night as so many other women likely had been based on his reputation. A ribbon of jealousy wound its way through her at that thought. She didn't want to be a number anymore. Even with Michael, she'd not been a one and only. That's what she wanted, to someday be so important to a man, to be so loved by him, that every other woman on the earth could fall away and he wouldn't notice. But she wondered if it was rarer than she'd ever imagined. After all, until recently she'd thought she was fortunate enough to have exactly that.

No, she refused to spend such a beautiful morning thinking about Michael. Instead, she watched yet another man she'd never be with and tried to imagine what it would be like if she could. As her fantasies ran wild, she thought about how Chloe would be shocked to know her best friend was wondering what her younger brother looked like naked.

When Owen reined the horse to a halt in front of her a few minutes later, she feared he could somehow read her thoughts, could see them in the way her face heated as if she'd just stepped into an oven.

"Looks like you've done a good job training her," she said.

"I hope so. I need to make this work." He swung out of the saddle and started leading the horse out of the corral toward the barn.

"I guess it's expensive to take care of a horse."

"It can be."

She sensed something else he wasn't saying, so she followed him into the barn, keeping a safe distance from Charlotte and her hooves. When he had the horse safely in the stall, Linnea watched as he brushed the animal. "Is something wrong?"

"No, I just need to prove I can do this." He shook his head as if he hadn't meant to say that.

"Don't you think you can?"

He met her eyes for a moment before refocusing on his task. "I do, but not everyone is so convinced. And I can't blame them. I've not exactly been Mr. Steady and Reliable over the years."

"So you've tried different things. Lots of people do that."

"And never stuck with any of them. They don't say much about my training, but I know they're all just waiting for me to lose interest in it, as well."

"Will you?"

This time when he met her gaze, he held it longer. "No. This feels different, like I've finally found what I was meant to do."

She shrugged. "Then who cares what other people think? I figure if you have to spend hours a day doing something to make a living, you ought to enjoy it. Too many people are stuck in jobs that they hate, and that's sad."

Owen stared at her as if he couldn't believe what she'd said. "Thanks."

"For what? Telling the truth?"

"For not doubting me."

"If you believe you can do this, then I don't have any right to doubt you. I know what it's like. When I wanted to open my own store right out of college, my dad cautioned me to work in someone else's shop first, see if I liked it. But I've known since I was a little girl what I wanted to do, ever since I was the flower girl in my cousin Jane's wedding."

"From what Chloe says, your shop is successful."

"I can't complain." Her doubts about going back in the wake of Michael's betrayal resurfaced, but she didn't want to think about that right now. She'd deal with it when the time came.

Owen set the brush aside and walked toward her. "Why wedding stuff? It all seems like such a huge waste of money. You only use it once."

"It's the allure of the fairy tale. Even independent women who can do fine on their own dream of happily ever after, and when they find it, they want their wedding to be perfect." She looked away and swallowed. "I wanted my wedding to be perfect, and it would have been if the groom hadn't turned out to be such a loser."

"It's good to see you angry about it."

She shifted her gaze back to him. "Why is that good?"

He reached out and brushed his fingertips across her cheek. "Because you're not crying anymore."

Linnea stood frozen, every bit of her mind focusing on the feel of his fingers. She should slip away from that touch, but it was as if she'd been ensnared by the gentleness of it. "I think I've shed enough tears over Michael Benson."

She'd like to believe that she truly was done with the tears, was determined to be, but she didn't know if the pain might hit her again out of the blue. Common sense told her you didn't get over losing the man you loved in a few days, but she kept telling herself that he didn't deserve her love, that he never had, and that she deserved to be able to move on.

Owen dropped his hand to the top of the stall. "You really do need to learn how to ride."

"About as much as I need to learn to ride a unicycle on a tightwire."

She could say the same thing about letting herself feel too much attraction toward Owen.

Before she did or said something she'd regret, she took a couple of steps back. "You know what's going to help more than getting on top of an animal that could stomp me into a squishy mess?"

"Mucking out the stalls for me?"

"Nice try." She glanced out the end of the barn. "No, I'm thinking retail therapy."

She'd spend Michael right out of her head. And maybe Owen while she was at it.

THANK GOD FOR women's need to shop. As Owen watched Linnea walk out of the barn, he was thankful females never had too many shoes in their closets. Because if Linnea hadn't left when she had, he had the horrible feeling he might have done something really, really dumb.

He ran his hand over his face, wondering where he'd misplaced his brain. Because making a move on his sister's best friend when she was still hurting from the mother of all breakups would definitely be his worst decision yet. And he had a life full of bad decisions.

And what was with the sudden attraction toward Linnea, anyway? He'd known her since he was a teenager. Yeah, he'd recognized she was pretty, but he'd been nothing but a giant walking hormone back then. Almost any girl he saw drew his interest.

He was beginning to think the giant walking hormone thing was making a comeback, because just skimming his fingers across her cheek had sent a shot of desire through him, enough that he'd been glad there was a stall hiding the effect it'd had on him.

What the hell was he thinking? Hadn't he learned his lesson about women with whom he had nothing in common? And he definitely had nothing in common with Linnea. She cried over a guy who'd treated her like dirt, made her living selling dresses that cost more than his first two trucks put together and knew about as much about ranch life as a fluffy poodle attempting to herd cattle. She might be from Texas, but the woman couldn't even ride a horse.

Not to mention the last thing she needed right now was another unavailable guy.

He finished mucking out the stalls, not allowing himself to watch as Linnea drove away from the ranch. When he was finished, he knew he should saddle up and head out to where his dad and Garrett were working. Instead, he walked back to Charlotte's stall and scratched her forehead. He allowed himself to replay Linnea's words in his head, her belief that he should do what made him happy. She was the only person who knew about his goals who hadn't looked as if his failure was all but certain, not an *if*, but a *when*. He knew his family loved him and their doubt was totally his fault. But that only made him want to prove himself even more.

And for some reason, he wanted to prove himself to Linnea, too. That, more than anything else, told him he needed to stay away from her, no matter that part of him wanted to do the exact opposite.

EVEN THOUGH SHE'D told Owen she was going to town for some retail therapy, Linnea hadn't meant to walk out of Merline Teague's art gallery with a painting. But the striking piece depicting a field of bluebonnets had captured her eye the moment she walked through the front door. She had no idea where she would hang it, but she hadn't been able to walk out the door without it.

"I hope you have a good rest of your visit," Merline said as she accompanied Linnea to the door and held it open for her.

"Thank you."

After she safely tucked her new purchase in the back of her car, she headed to the Primrose Café to have lunch with Chloe and some of her friends.

"Hey, Lin." Chloe waved to her as soon as she stepped in the front door.

Linnea headed over to the table in the corner where Chloe sat with four other women. She knew Keri Teague, one of Merline's daughters-in-law, who owned the Mehlerhaus

Bakery. And she'd briefly met Elissa Kayne, India Parrish and Skyler Bradshaw during a couple of other visits to Blue Falls.

"So, have you bought out the town yet?" Chloe asked as Linnea slid onto the empty chair next to her friend.

"She better not have," India said. "She hasn't been to my store yet."

Linnea smiled along with the rest of the women. "I think there might still be a little bit of room on my credit card."

"Good. Because I have the perfect dress for you."

They halted their conversation when the waitress walked up to the table to take their orders. As the pretty young woman wrote on her notepad, Linnea couldn't help but notice that there was sadness in her eyes.

When she walked away, Linnea watched her. "Is she okay?"

At the uncomfortable silence, Linnea shifted her attention to her lunch companions.

"Suffering from a broken heart, I'm afraid," India said.

That's why Linnea had picked up on it so quickly. Birds of a feather. "Lot of that going around."

The other women looked a little uncomfortable, making it obvious that they knew what had happened to her. Chloe had probably planned this cheer-up lunch the moment she'd found out Linnea had come to town.

"Maybe we should fix up Tara with one of your brothers," Elissa said.

"She's already been out with Owen once," Chloe said.

"Everyone's been out with Owen once," Keri said. "It's his magic number."

Chloe swatted Keri on her arm. "Hey, that's my baby brother you're talking about."

Keri's gaze shifted to Chloe. "Tell me I'm wrong."

Chloe sighed, unable to refute Keri's characterization.

Linnea thought back to how Owen had caressed her cheek earlier, how he'd held her hand in the truck the night before, how nice and caring he'd been since she arrived. Something unwanted twisted inside her at the thought that he'd done the same thing, probably more, with countless other women. What was wrong with her that it bothered her at all?

"You okay, Lin?" Chloe asked.

"Sorry, we shouldn't be talking about this," Keri said.

Linnea waved away their concern. "It's okay. Not like I'm going to be able to go through the rest of my life without running into people who've had their hearts broken."

India reached over and patted Linnea's hand.

"I know it's hard right now, but you'll find someone else."

"I'm going to guess that the only thing Linnea is interested in doing with a man now is stringing one up by his tender bits," Elissa said.

Linnea hadn't expected to laugh in the middle of the current conversation, but that's exactly what she did. "I think that's the best idea I've heard all day."

They fell into conversation about their families, their businesses and, unfortunately, Owen's penchant for serial dating, pausing only when Tara delivered their meals.

"I think the only person who has him beat is Greg Bozeman," Keri said. "If that man ever settles down, we'll know hell is about to become an ice-skating rink."

"Maybe they just haven't found the right women to make them settle down yet," Chloe said as she picked up one of her fries.

There was a momentary pause before everyone else at the table started laughing. Linnea didn't really know Greg Bozeman, but she had to shove down the desire to defend Owen, to say that he was a good person who had plans for his life, that he was more than a guy who hopped from one woman's bed to the next. Only for all she knew, that was how he managed his love life. It shouldn't matter to her, but she found herself hoping it wasn't true. And not for her sake but for his. Somehow in the past few days, she felt as if she'd seen beyond the Owen whom most people saw to a hint of the man beneath the surface, and that man deserved more than empty dalliances.

She shook her head as she realized her years of selling happily ever after had to be messing with how she viewed people. Maybe not everyone was cut out for happily ever after. Maybe she wasn't.

"So, how long are you in town?" Skyler asked as she picked at her salad.

"I don't know. I should really head back home, but I haven't been able to face that quite yet." She lowered her fork to her plate, her appetite draining away. "Honestly, I'm having a hard time thinking about even going back to Dallas."

"Maybe you don't have to," Keri said.

"I don't really have a choice. I've got a business to run."

"From what Chloe says, the business is doing well. Maybe it's time to expand, open a second location."

"Oh, Lin, you could stay here," Chloe said, her eyes alight with excitement. "It would be great to see you all the time instead of every few months."

"I don't know. That's a lot to consider." And she wasn't exactly in the best mental state for making huge decisions.

"Sometimes a fresh start is exactly what a person needs," Keri said. "It did wonders for both my sisters-in-law. You should talk to

Grace. She had a business in Arkansas, but she's made the transition to Blue Falls."

Linnea was surprised by how much she was intrigued by the idea. In fact, an unexpected wave of excitement ran through her.

"Oh, my God. I just had the best idea," India said. "The store space two doors down from Keri's bakery has been empty for only a couple of weeks now. If you took over that, maybe you and Keri could work in conjunction. You'd take care of dressing the bridal party, do the china and crystal, all that fun stuff."

"And I could do the cakes." Keri clapped her hands once. "I love it."

Chloe pointed at Elissa. "You could do the flowers." Her finger shifted toward Skyler. "And weddings could be held at the inn, or at least the guests could stay there."

"I could possibly dress the mother of the bride or the bride's traveling attire for after the reception. This all just seems meant to be," India said.

Elissa leaned back in her chair. "That just leaves Chloe."

Chloe shrugged. "I could always hand out valium for nerves."

That caused even more laughter, and though she felt as if she'd been caught up in a whirlwind, Linnea had to admit the excitement was rubbing off on her, as well. Could she really make that big a change? Would it work financially? Maybe now, when her life was already racked with upheaval, was the best time to really examine where she was in her life, where she wanted to go, and which path to take.

Tara came back to the table and left their checks. Seeing her reminded Linnea of Owen, and a huge sliver of doubt wormed its way through the excitement. If she moved to Blue Falls, would her silly infatuation with Owen go away? Or would it just get worse? Did she want to risk finding out?

"I bet you could look at the space this afternoon if you wanted to," Keri said.

Linnea held up her hand. "I need to think about this first. It feels a little like a runaway train at the moment."

"You're right, of course," India said. "We kind of get carried away sometimes. Sorry about that."

"No need to apologize. I'll admit, the idea is intriguing. I just… With everything that's happened I don't want to make any rash decisions."

Even though she was urging herself to use caution, her excitement grew as they finished their lunches and conversation shifted to other things she had trouble concentrating on. Before the revelation of Michael's lies, she could never have imagined walking away from her shop, from her home in Dallas. But now it appealed to her on so many levels. Her mind started running wild with ideas, of how she would design a new store differently. By the time lunch was winding down, she'd changed her mind.

She looked at Keri and said, "You know, I think I will look at that space after all."

When she walked into the empty building an hour later, the sound of her feet echoing against the wooden floor, she thought maybe she'd lost all her common sense. Because she fell in love with the space instantly, even though it was totally different from the posh interior of her Dallas shop. Maybe that's what appealed to her, that it was a total departure from what she was used to. If she was going to make a change in her life, why not go big?

Her rational side tried to take over, but she shoved it away. Even if she didn't go through with making the move, she wanted a few minutes to fantasize what it would be like.

"It's awesome, right?" Keri said as she and

the rest of her friends filed into the empty storefront behind Linnea.

"Yeah." And it was. Linnea walked toward the back, admiring the historic feel of the building. In addition to the wooden floors, the crystal chandeliers, copper ceiling and lengthy glass countertops in antique cabinetry made the space rich with potential. She loved the idea of mixing the feel of Texas history with modern wedding finery. For the first time since she'd left Dallas, she experienced some of the familiar excitement about her chosen profession. Her love life might be in shambles, but part of her still believed in happily ever after. At least for some people.

Justine, the real estate agent, pointed out stairs in the back. "Would you like to see the upstairs?"

Linnea nodded, a new wave of excitement filling her at the thought of all the extra space she could have here, more than twice what her shop had in Dallas. But could she make it work? Blue Falls might draw a fair amount of tourist traffic, but would they come there to get married? Her Dallas shop might be smaller, but it was well placed for brides looking for more than a chain-store bridal experience.

If she'd harbored a thought that the upstairs might dampen her enthusiasm for the building, one look proved her wrong. The walls were exposed brick with a lot of character, and the tall windows facing the street let in streams of gorgeous natural light. She ran her fingers along the brick as she walked toward the front to look out one of the twin windows. From that vantage point, she could see India's store, Yesterwear, across the street as well as several other businesses. This was a perfect location right in the heart of a bustling little tourist town, and the idea of working with the other women to build Blue Falls into a wedding destination made her creative neurons spark like firecrackers.

Chloe came to stand next to her. "So, what do you think?"

"Honestly, I love it and feel ready to jump at the opportunity right this minute, which is what scares me."

"How so?"

"I can't say that I really trust my own judgment at this point."

"This isn't the same thing."

"No, but am I just running away from my problems instead of facing them head-on?"

Chloe sighed. "I can't answer that."

No, only Linnea could. But at the moment she couldn't, and that sent up all kinds of caution flags that she shouldn't be making any big, life-altering decisions while her emotions were still so raw and confused.

Even so, that didn't alleviate the sense of loss when she stepped out of the building back onto the sidewalk. She couldn't believe how hard it was to resist the pull of leaping into the change headfirst. It just felt right. But so had saying yes to Michael's proposal. She wasn't willing to let her years of hard work go down the same drain as her love life, no matter how much she wanted to say yes yet again.

Chapter Six

Despite telling herself repeatedly that she needed to approach any big decisions slowly and with a lot of caution, she couldn't stop the flood of ideas her visit to the empty store space had started. She told herself that it was okay to fantasize, that perhaps she could even take some of the new ideas and apply them to her shop in Dallas.

As she pulled into the drive leading onto the ranch, she was glad she'd talked herself into a day in town. Granted, her fluttery feelings around Owen had prompted it, but she felt better than she had since Michael's duplicity was revealed. She even started humming a song she'd heard in Yesterwear, where she'd bought herself the pretty new dress that India had said would be perfect for her. As she'd watched India working with customers to match them with the perfect outfits, she felt they were kindred spirits.

She had to admit that being able to hang out with Chloe, India and the rest of their group of friends was another plus in Blue Falls' favor. But it wasn't as if she didn't have friends in Dallas, Katrina chief among them. But as much as she loved Katrina, they didn't hang out that often outside of work. She could absolutely imagine regular lunches with the Blue Falls crew. There was just something about this little slice of the Hill Country and the people in it that made her believe she could move beyond her heartbreak.

She glanced toward the barn as she parked, trying not to think that some part of her subconscious might be considering Owen as a mark on the plus side of the "move to Blue Falls" pros-and-cons list. Thankfully, his truck was gone, giving her more time to shake the feelings he'd elicited earlier.

As she got out of her car and walked to the back to retrieve her painting, she heard an engine slowing before turning into the driveway. Her heart sped up at the thought of seeing Owen again. Maybe she should heed that reaction more than anything else as a sign that she should put all the nonsense about moving to Blue Falls and starting over out of her mind and get back to real life in Dallas.

But as she pulled the painting from the trunk, she realized the vehicle drawing near didn't sound like Owen's truck. Or any of the other vehicles she'd heard coming and going at the ranch since her arrival. When she glanced over her shoulder, she nearly dropped the painting.

Panic rose like bile in her throat, threatening

to choke her, as she recognized the black SUV. She wanted to run into the house and hide until Michael went away, the same as she had done the day his wife delivered her life-shattering news. But he evidently wasn't going to give up until she told him face-to-face that she never wanted to see him again. She'd never once been scared of Michael, but his determination to find her coupled with the fact that she was alone at the ranch caused a swell of unease in her.

When he stepped out onto the dusty drive in his expensive leather shoes and crisply pressed pants, he looked more out of place than a ballerina at a biker bar.

"Thank goodness I finally found you," he said as he walked toward her.

Linnea refused to retreat, but she did place the painting between them at an angle that forced him to stay a few feet away. "Why are you here?" Even though her insides were churning, she managed to keep any hint of upset out of her voice.

"We need to talk."

"No, we don't."

"You haven't answered any of my calls."

The way he was acting like the injured party made anger bubble up in her chest. "Perhaps that's because I blocked your number. And maybe you need to learn to take a hint."

"You need to let me explain."

"Is that right? I don't think there's any way for you to explain the fact that you planned to marry me while you were already married."

Beyond Michael, Linnea caught sight of another vehicle popping over the hill in the road. Her heart leaped as she realized it was Owen's truck pulling a horse trailer. Part of her wanted to sigh in relief, but another didn't want him to cross paths with Michael, not after he'd offered to give Michael a good beating. She wanted Michael to really listen to her and leave, even if a small part of her knew it was going to hurt all over again to watch him drive away.

"I know I messed up, but I'm here to make it all up to you. I left Danielle and filed for divorce. We can be together now just like we planned."

She just stared at him as Owen drove past them toward the barn. "I think you missed the part where the divorce should have come first before you nearly made me into a bigamist."

"I made a mistake, but I know you still love me. Otherwise, you wouldn't have run to the middle of nowhere because I'd hurt you."

He didn't actually turn up his nose at the ranch, but she heard it in his voice. "I came to the ranch because I didn't want to see you ever again."

"You don't mean that." He sounded so condescending, as if she were a little woman who didn't know her own mind. She couldn't believe what she was hearing. It was as if he were a different person. Not once in the months she'd known him had he attempted to make her feel small and stupid, but he was certainly in that ballpark now. Not that she was going to allow it.

"I assure you, I mean every word. Now, I want you to turn around and leave, and never contact me again." She turned for the house, not wanting to have to look at him one second longer.

Michael grabbed her arm, startling a gasp out of her. His fingers dug into her flesh.

"Let me go right now."

"I'm not done talking."

"You'd better do as she says." Owen's voice was deadly calm, but when Linnea looked at him approaching she saw a fury burning in his eyes.

"Move along, cowboy. This isn't your business."

"If you don't remove your hand from Lin's arm and step away, you're going to wish you had."

At first, Linnea didn't think Michael was going to heed Owen's warning. But then he must have scraped together a few shreds of common sense and released her.

Michael's mouth pressed into a tight line as he stared at Owen. Then he shifted his gaze to Linnea. "So he's the reason you're avoiding me. How long have you been shacking up with him?"

Owen moved toward Michael so fast that Linnea barely had time to step between them and press her hand firmly against Owen's chest.

"Don't. He's just trying to get a rise out of you."

"Well, it's working."

"He's not worth it."

She glanced over her shoulder in time to see a satisfied smirk on Michael's face. It was almost enough to convince her to let Owen deliver on his promise of pummeling her ex. But Michael was a man with means, connections, and she refused to be the reason he targeted Owen or any of the rest of the Brodys. When she was reasonably certain Owen wasn't going to attack Michael, she turned around to face the man she'd almost married. Standing there looking at what must be the real Michael Benson, she couldn't believe she'd ever even been attracted to him, let alone loved him.

"If you don't leave within the next thirty seconds, I'm going to call the sheriff to remove you forcibly."

Despite her threat, he stared at her for several seconds. "You'll come to your senses soon."

"I already have."

She stood her ground until his vehicle made the turn onto the road and he gunned it toward town. Only then did the shaking start. That's also when she realized she'd been holding onto the painting during the entire altercation. Her tight grip on it faltered, and she dropped it into the dirt.

Owen steadied her, one hand on her back and the other on her arm. "You okay?"

Her head swam. "I think I need to sit."

Owen guided her to the porch steps and eased her down before kneeling in front of her. He framed the left side of her face with his hand. "Did he hurt you?"

It took her a moment to settle on an answer. In truth, she could still feel the bite of his fingers digging into her arm, but she didn't want to say anything that might send Owen racing after him. "No, I'm fine."

Owen's eyes narrowed a fraction as if he knew she was lying. "I shouldn't have left you alone."

"It's not your fault. I wasn't even here when you left, and I never imagined he'd show up." She glanced toward the road, half afraid Michael would return. "I know you might not believe this, but I've never seen him like that. It was as if I was witnessing a Jekyll and Hyde thing."

"People don't always show their true colors."

There was more behind those words than trying to make her feel better. "You sound like you're speaking from experience."

"Maybe I am."

Was it possible that someone had hurt Owen? He was so happy-go-lucky and known for being a class-A flirt that she'd never considered he'd ever loved and lost. Chloe hadn't said anything about Owen being serious about anyone, but maybe she didn't know.

Instead of asking, however, she shifted her gaze to the trailer behind his truck. A chocolate-brown horse had its head stuck out on one side. "You got another horse."

"Yeah. I've had my eye on him for a while. I think he'll make a good mount for a roper."

When she glanced at Owen, it was almost as

if she could see the gears working in his head. "You really like evaluating horses, don't you?"

His gaze connected with hers. "What makes you say that?"

"The look you get on your face, sort of a mixture between excitement and like you're running complex mathematical equations in your head."

He laughed. "I guarantee it's not the latter. Just ask Mrs. Johnston, my high school algebra teacher. I think she might have thrown a party when I passed her class."

She smiled, imagining Owen fidgeting in a class like that. She honestly had a hard time seeing him being able to stay inside long enough to complete a full day of school. He was as much a part of the Texas landscape, in her mind, as live oak trees, mesquite and a hot western wind.

"I don't know a lot about horses, but I'm going to assume it takes a different type of animal for rodeo than what you'd want for working on the ranch. How'd you get interested in rodeo animals?"

His eyes narrowed a fraction. "Are you sure you want to talk about this right now after what just happened?"

Unconsciously, she touched her arm where Michael's fingers had dug into her flesh. "Honestly, I'd like to talk about anything but what just happened. I'd like to forget it."

"I understand, but I don't like the fact that he came all this way and thought he could manhandle you."

"I let him know I wasn't interested anymore, so he should stay away now." She wanted to believe that, didn't want to think that the man she'd been head over heels in love with might cause her harm. Deep down she wasn't so sure, but she hoped that was only her insecurity whispering to her and not an actual threat.

Owen reached over and wrapped his hand around hers. She tried not to think about how much she liked the strong, work-roughened feel of it. Still, she found herself hoping he didn't release her any time soon. While she was typically very independent and capable of taking care of herself, Michael's appearance had shaken her and she latched onto the protected feeling she got sitting next to Owen.

"So, the rodeo stock?"

Owen ran his thumb across her knuckles as he glanced toward the horse trailer. "I rode the amateur rodeo circuit for a while. I enjoyed it, but not enough to really do it full-time and try to make the big time. I was waiting my turn to ride one night when I started assessing the strengths and weaknesses of all the other riders' horses. That's when I realized I was more interested in the animals than riding them."

"Makes sense that you'd like animals, since you grew up on a ranch."

"Yeah, but the focus here has always been more on the cattle, not the horses."

"Maybe you can change that, diversify."

He stopped his absent rubbing of her hand and looked straight into her eyes. "That's exactly what I want to do. It makes more financial sense to me."

"Plus, it's something that actually interests you."

"Don't get me wrong. I love the ranch. It's home."

She placed her hand atop his. "Owen, you don't have to explain to me. There's nothing wrong with wanting to forge your own path. I actually think it's smart—for your happiness as well as financially."

Linnea noticed the look of surprise on his face. "What?"

"You're amazing."

Those two words sent a wave of warmth through her, making her smile. "I can't imagine why."

"Because most women would be sitting here

freaking out about Michael right now. Instead, you're able to see something no one ever has."

"Well, first off, freaking out isn't going to do me any good at all. And I'm sure your family knows what your dream is and supports it."

"Maybe on some level, but you seem like you believe I might actually succeed."

"Why would I believe otherwise? The world is full of stories of people finding their passion and turning it into successful business ventures."

He looked as though he was on the verge of saying something else when the sound of an engine caught their attention. Linnea hated to admit it, but a moment of panic welled within her. Owen must have felt her tense, because he squeezed her hand.

"It's only Chloe." With that realization, he released her and stood. "If you're okay, I better unload the horse and get him situated in the barn."

"I'm fine, thanks."

Owen's eyes met hers again, and her heart fluttered.

"No, thank you," he said.

She was so busy telling herself to look away from him as he turned and walked toward the barn that it took her several seconds to realize how much feeling he'd put into that thank-you. Did he really not think anyone believed in him? Was he right?

Chloe pulled to a quick stop not far from the porch and hopped out of her car. As she approached, Linnea saw what looked like concern on her face.

"You saw Michael, didn't you?"

Chloe stopped in her tracks. "Yes, he came to the clinic, wanted me to 'talk some sense into you,'" she said, using air quotes. "Lin, he…"

"Didn't seem like the same man who proposed to me? Yeah, I know."

"Are you okay? He sort of freaked me out."

"You're not the only one." Linnea glanced toward the barn, where Owen was leading the new horse out of the trailer. She might be afraid to get too close to the animals, but she knew a gorgeous piece of horseflesh when she saw it. And a gorgeous man, too. "Luckily, Owen got home when he did."

"You were here alone when Michael showed up?"

"Briefly. But I'm okay. He's gone, hopefully for good." She realized she'd been staring at Owen too long when Chloe went quiet, so she shifted her attention to her friend.

Chloe glanced toward her brother before eyeing Linnea. "Is something going on?"

Linnea searched for a plausible explanation for why she'd been staring at Owen. "I just have conflicted feelings about what happened. I don't like to be the type of woman who depends on a man, but I can't deny that I felt safer when your brother drove up."

Chloe seemed to accept the explanation. "You know Owen and Garrett would do anything for you. You've always been like another sister to them."

That was nice, but Linnea hadn't been thinking sisterly thoughts toward the youngest Brody sibling. In the depths of her own mind she could acknowledge that as she'd watched him walk toward the barn, she was wondering what it would be like to strip his clothes off and take a proverbial roll in the hay.

She stood before Chloe could see the rush of heat invading her cheeks. "I need to go check in with Katrina."

"Okay, but if you need anything, even just to talk, call me."

"I will. Sorry you came over here for nothing."

"Don't be silly. I have to make sure my bestie doesn't need me to open up a can of whoop-ass."

Linnea laughed at Chloe's fighter stance. "I think you'd scare him off just doing that." She gestured toward Chloe's raised fists and leg seemingly ready to do a side kick. "What is that, anyway?"

Chloe lowered her leg to the ground. "Okay, so maybe I'd just run over him with my car."

Linnea thought she'd dealt with Michael's disturbing appearance at the ranch pretty well until she was alone in the guest bedroom a few minutes later. The shaking started again, and she hugged herself and paced to try to make it stop. Never could she have imagined she would be worried about being alone with Michael. Only a short time ago, it had been the perfect way to end a long day. She stared at herself in the full-length mirror and shook her head. How could she have gotten it so wrong with him?

To try to take her mind off Michael, she called Katrina to check how things were going. After they talked business for a few minutes, Linnea sensed Katrina was holding something back.

"What is it?"

"I sold your dress this morning."

Even though Linnea had been the one to tell Katrina to sell it as quickly as she could, the news still felt like a punch in the chest. She didn't need or even want it or Michael anymore. It was just one more thread severed from the life she'd thought she was about to embark on.

It was time to chart a new course. Did that include making the move to Blue Falls? Or did it show more strength to return to Dallas and get on with the business of living the life she'd built there?

Linnea stared out the window toward the barn, but Owen wasn't where she could see him. That was probably a good thing. She didn't need a good-looking cowboy clouding her already compromised judgment.

Katrina didn't ask when Linnea was coming back to work, and Linnea didn't offer, because she honestly didn't know. All she knew was that just thinking about the shop space in downtown Blue Falls was exciting. So was remembering what Owen looked like coming to her defense—fierce, determined, strong and sexy as hell.

After ending the call, she leaned her forehead against the windowpane. No matter how hard she tried, she couldn't stop thinking about Owen and the feel of his hand on her cheek, holding her hand, wrapping her in his arms so she could cry out her pain. Her mind was telling her that she needed to push all thoughts of Owen Brody away, but her body wasn't getting the message. Whether it was just a reaction to having her plans for happiness shattered or a genuine attraction, she wanted to find out what Owen was hiding underneath those Wranglers.

Chapter Seven

The new horse tossed his head, as if to show how annoyed he was by Owen's clumsy efforts to get him unsaddled. Owen couldn't blame the animal. His mind had been about as far away from training as possible as he'd ridden through some mock roping runs. His gaze had kept going to the house and the road, making sure Michael didn't return.

He'd allowed Linnea to stop him from slugging Michael earlier, but he still burned with the need to do exactly that. The ass deserved it for how he'd treated Linnea.

But it wasn't just chivalry and protectiveness

making him stick around the main part of the ranch instead of riding out to meet up with Garrett and his dad. Something new and honestly a little scary was stirring inside him every time he was around Linnea. It was as if he was seeing her with a different set of eyes, ones that looked beyond the fact that he'd known her for years to the fact that she was a beautiful, desirable woman. To be honest, he'd been fighting off that desire since she went into the house. It was a small miracle she hadn't noticed the effect being near her had on him when they were sitting on the front steps. Add in that she evidently believed he'd be successful in his horse training venture, and damn if he hadn't wanted to carry her inside straight to his bed.

He shook his head as he led Galahad, the new horse, into an empty stall. Thinking about Linnea as he would other women he wanted to take to bed was a very bad idea. But something tickled his brain at that thought. Linnea wasn't like other women. Not that he dated airheaded bimbos, but she was just a class above. Even in jeans and T-shirts, Linnea had that stylish-without-trying look about her.

Garrett and his dad walked into the barn leading their horses. As his dad drew near and spotted Galahad, he nodded once.

"I guess I know why you didn't turn up today."

"He's just still pouting because of the dump in the mud the other day," Garrett said as he bumped shoulders with Owen.

Normally, their teasing wouldn't bother him, but today he had to bite his tongue before he said something he'd regret. "Actually, I didn't want to leave Linnea alone here. Michael made an unannounced visit."

"Is she okay?" his dad asked.

Owen gripped the top of Galahad's stall until his knuckles turned white. "Yeah, but I'm not sure things would have ended as well if I hadn't shown up when I did."

"He threatened her?" Garrett's voice tensed, and Owen could tell his brother would punch Michael just as quickly as he would if necessary.

"Not in so many words, but I didn't like how he talked to her and he grabbed her arm."

"Good thing you stayed here, then," their dad said.

"Think we should call Simon?" Garrett asked, referring to Simon Teague, the local sheriff.

"Linnea said she didn't think he'd be back, but I'm not sure she believed what she was saying."

Their dad fiddled with his horse's reins, seeming to be deep in thought. "We'll leave it up to her for now, but we need to keep an eye out."

Owen nodded, then extended his hands to take the horses' reins. "I'll take care of them."

His dad paused in front of Galahad's stall.

"Fine-looking animal." But he headed out of the barn without saying anything about why Owen had bought the horse.

He sighed. Even with the knowledge that he'd not given his family much of a reason to believe in his sticking power, he couldn't deny he kept hoping they'd see he'd changed. Hadn't he?

At least Linnea saw it. Or she acted as though she did.

He really should go into town and find a way to alleviate some tension, get Linnea off his mind. That was his plan all the way through dinner. He did his best to ignore the concern that Linnea thought she was hiding, but his gaze kept going to her. He imagined taking care of Michael Benson so she'd never have to worry about him again. And despite trying to force himself to think about whom he might hook up with if he went out for a couple of beers, his imagination kept going back to Linnea and how she'd look with that long red hair flowing down over her bare shoulders.

Garrett swatted him on the arm.

He jerked his attention to his older brother. "What the hell?"

"Come back from la-la land and pass the beans."

Owen resisted the urge to flip Garrett the bird and handed over the bowl of green beans.

"You don't have to make dinner for us," his dad said to Linnea.

"And you know I'm not about to stay here and twiddle my thumbs." She smiled, and Owen wondered if anyone but he could see how much effort it took.

His dad patted Linnea's hand. "I'd adopt you if I didn't think your parents would fight me over you."

She made a dismissive gesture. "Ah, they wouldn't miss me. They've got two other daughters, and one of them is about to give them a grandbaby. Can't compete with that."

The image of Linnea's stomach rounded with a child hit Owen's brain with enough force that he choked on his green beans. He coughed so hard that his eyes watered. By the time he got his lungs under control, everyone else was staring at him. The depth of the concern in Linnea's beautiful eyes nearly made him choke again. He pulled his gaze away from her.

"Went down the wrong way."

"Killer green beans," Garrett said. "Got it."

Owen smacked Garrett on the back of the head.

Their dad sighed and glanced at Linnea. "I keep thinking they'll grow up someday."

This time her smile was more genuine. "I don't know. They are entertaining."

Owen thought Linnea might be feeling better, but after dinner when his dad offered to get out some cards for a game of poker, she passed, saying she wanted to go enjoy the night air.

All through his turn at washing the dishes, Owen worried about Linnea being outside alone. The moment he was done, he slipped out the back door to make sure she was safe.

When he didn't immediately see her, panic threatened. She wasn't on the front porch or standing next to the pasture fence. His heart hammering, he hurried toward the barn despite her professed fear of horses. He cursed when he didn't see her inside, either. Damn it, he should have accompanied her outside even if she had wanted to be alone. He ran out of the barn, already planning how to kill Michael if he'd hurt her.

"Linnea," he called out.

"Yeah?"

He spun on his heel to find her emerging out of the dark. "Damn, woman. You scared me half to death."

"Sorry."

He closed the distance between them and placed his hands on her shoulders. "I thought Michael had come back."

She reached behind her and pulled a steak knife from her back jeans pocket. "I didn't come unprepared."

He cursed. "What if he'd used that on you?"

"I was careful. I just needed some fresh air to think. I've got a lot on my mind." She shoved the knife back into her pocket and walked over to the fence, close to where they'd stood and talked before. "I should get back to Dallas."

A visceral need to talk her out of that surprised Owen, almost as much as the vision of her pregnant at dinner. He so needed a drink. "Isn't Katrina holding down the fort for you?"

"Yes, but I can't hide from my life forever. And I feel awful that I brought my troubles to your doorstep."

"I think we can handle one jackass."

"But you shouldn't have to." She turned toward him, making him aware of how close she was, close enough for him to pull her into his arms and kiss her.

No longer able to keep his hands off her, he caressed her cheek. "And you shouldn't have to go back before you're ready."

She looked so lost, so conflicted that it tore at his heart.

"Lin?"

She lifted her gaze to his, and her lips parted slightly. He saw a hint of encouragement in her eyes, enough to shatter his self-control. He lowered his mouth to hers, tasting the cherry pie they'd had for dessert on her lips. When her hands drifted up his chest, he wrapped his arms around her and pulled her close to deepen the kiss. She felt so good in his arms, a perfect fit.

That thought shot a bolt of common sense to his otherwise drugged brain, and he broke the kiss and stepped away from her.

"What's wrong?" she asked, a little breathless.

"I can't do this."

She took a couple of breaths and looked as if she was having a debate with herself. "Why not?"

"Because we're friends. You're my sister's best friend." He ran his hand over his face. "And it's wrong to take advantage of you after what you've been through."

"It didn't feel like you were taking advantage of me."

"Lin, you know me. I'm a play-the-field kind of guy. No serious, long-term relationships." He'd learned his lesson when he'd given his heart to someone only to have it discarded like an unwanted gift.

"I can't say I'm a fan of serious relationships, either, at the moment." Linnea watched him as if she was wrestling with a decision. "I don't think that's what I want right now."

He relaxed a little. "Good. We're on the same page."

But then she took a step toward him, looking nervous and excited at the same time. What the...? He wasn't one to walk away from a willing woman most of the time, but this was different.

"Lin, you're not thinking straight."

"I'm not looking for forever." She placed her hand tentatively against his chest.

Though it pained him to do so, he grasped her hand and pulled it away before he did something irreversible. "You're not a fling sort of woman."

She looked up at him, and he saw a yearning in her eyes that was going to be damn hard to resist if he didn't get her back inside where his dad and Garrett could serve as a barrier.

"Maybe a fling is exactly what I need."

The woman was trying to kill him.

"I think we should go back inside."

"Why?" She took a deep breath. "We're both adults, Owen." She paused again before continuing. "Ones with needs."

He shook his head. "There are other ways to deal with those needs. Trust me."

Linnea lowered her gaze. "I'm sorry. I evidently read things wrong."

As she started to turn away, a part of him couldn't let her feel like she was being rejected again, especially not when her thinking he wasn't attracted to her would be a lie. He grabbed her hand, causing her to return her gaze to his. "You didn't read it wrong, but we can't. Chloe would kill me for taking advantage of you when you're still hurting about Michael."

She winced at the sound of the other man's name. "Or maybe she'd be angry with me for seducing her baby brother. But Chloe doesn't have to know."

Linnea licked her lips as if she were already anticipating the taste of him, and he went rock hard. He had to fight the image of taking her up against the side of the barn.

"Trust me, if we gave in to this, you'd regret it." Never had he tried so hard to convince a woman she didn't want to make love to him.

Though his body was screaming at him that he was the king of idiots, he walked away.

LINNEA STARED OUT the window of India's boutique, watching people come and go and eyeing the empty store space across the street. She thought about how making a move and starting over had been as big a pipe dream as the one she'd had about spending the rest of her life happily married to Michael. But how could she move to Blue Falls now when she'd made such a fool of herself the night before? She still couldn't believe she'd actually told Owen she wanted to have a fling with him.

And she'd realized how uncomfortable she'd made him when Garrett was the one hanging around the ranch today instead of his younger brother. So when India had called to ask if she would come speak to the latest BlueBelles class, part of a series aimed at arming young girls with tools for a successful life, she'd jumped at the chance.

India and Skyler said goodbye to the last of the girls, then walked over to where Linnea was standing.

"Thank you again for saving our bacon," India said. "I thought Skyler and I were going to have to resort to song and dance when our speaker canceled last minute."

Skyler laughed. "You would have been on your own there."

Linnea smiled. "I was glad to help, for whatever it was worth."

India leaned on the rack of blouses and skirts inspired by the Roaring Twenties. "Are you kidding? You were fabulous. It's so important to teach young girls to reach for their dreams and believe in themselves, and you did exactly that."

"I halfway want to open a wedding gown shop after listening to you," Skyler said, drawing a small laugh from Linnea.

India pointed out the window. "You thought any more about taking that space?"

"Some." She'd told the girls in the BlueBelles class that they shouldn't let obstacles or fears derail them from the paths to their dreams. As she looked across the street, she realized she'd been doing exactly that. She'd been telling herself that even considering moving her store, or opening a second location, was letting Michael win. But as she sifted through her feelings, not taking the space because of Owen felt more like a cop-out.

"And?"

"Still thinking. Honestly, I was afraid I was only looking at the space as a way to get away from Michael and all the bad memories. But I don't think that's it."

"You really like it, can see its potential," India said.

"Yeah."

"Even though it's been hurt, I still say to go with where your heart is pointing you."

An image of Owen Brody popped into her mind, but she did her best to shove it aside. She wanted to make the decision about the store without even considering Michael, Owen or any other man. This decision was for her and what would make her happy.

"Not to push you," Skyler said, "but I do know that Justine has shown the building to several other potential buyers. She said one of them seemed pretty serious. Some guy who owns a couple of other antiques malls."

The way Skyler said "antiques malls" made Linnea picture one of those cluttered places filled with old junk, not things that were actually antiques. Not that poking through those types of stores couldn't be fun, but it just didn't fit with the feel of Blue Falls' downtown area. And it would be a shame to cover up all that gorgeous space with a warren of dusty trinkets.

When she left Yesterwear, she headed for her car parked down the street. But the next thing she knew she was walking into the real estate office and asking Justine Ware a million questions about the empty building, how serious the other interested parties were and how long Justine thought Linnea had to make a decision before someone else committed to buy the property.

After she finished talking to Justine, she stopped by the Mehlerhaus Bakery.

"Hey," Keri said when Linnea walked into the bakery. "Did I just see you come out of the real estate office?"

"I did."

Keri leaned her arms against the top of the

glass-fronted counter full of delicious calories. "Does that mean you're going to take the empty store?"

"I'm leaning that way, but I have to do some financial calculations first, talk to my bank." She pointed toward the sweet treats. "Give me one of those lemon tarts."

When she tried to pay for her purchase, Keri waved away Linnea's money. "It's on the house."

"Thank you. So, were you serious when you said you'd like to work together on weddings?"

"Absolutely. And I know India and Skyler were, too. I even know a photographer we might rope into joining forces."

A burst of excitement nearly had Linnea's imagination off and running, but she had to reclaim rational thought. Expanding her business was a huge step, not something she could just do on a whim like when she'd fled Dallas for some emotional healing at the Brody ranch.

"I'm trying not to get ahead of myself, but I have to admit the ideas are flowing like crazy in my head."

"Good. Maybe those ideas will convince you this is the right thing to do."

It was difficult to keep the excitement of a new venture quelled so that she could look at her options rationally, especially when Justine let her into the building again so she could take pictures and notes. By the time she got back to the ranch and spent a couple of hours making pros-and-cons lists, sketches of possible layouts for a showroom and even marking down ideas for an apartment on the top floor, she realized she needed to talk to Katrina. After all, she was a partner in the Dallas store. Granted, Linnea owned the majority share, but Katrina still had a say in business decisions of this size.

She'd been sitting so long that she needed to get up and stretch her legs. When she glanced out the kitchen window, she spotted Owen working with the new horse he'd brought home when Michael was making his unwelcome appearance. As she watched Owen put the animal through its paces, she couldn't help but notice how good Owen looked. He used his legs more than the reins to guide the animal, and she wondered how strong those legs would feel entwined with hers. Heat flooded her entire body, and an ache to be held, to have her desires sated, settled deep and low inside her.

As she'd told Owen, they were adults. They could satisfy their urges without any serious entanglements. She wasn't looking for a trip down the aisle, and she couldn't imagine he was, either. Maybe he had the right idea, to keep sexual relationships free and easy. But he'd made his stance on them getting involved clear.

Feeling antsy, she called Chloe.

"Hey, I heard the BlueBelles class went well this morning," Chloe said.

Linnea pulled her gaze away from Owen

before she stalked outside and accosted him. "Yeah. Listen, any chance I can pull you away from your husband tonight?"

"Maybe. You want to do something?"

"Yeah. Girls' night. Maybe ask the other old married ladies to join us for some dancing."

"Even though I object to the term 'old married lady,' that sounds like a good idea."

When she walked into the living room an hour later dressed in the best outfit she'd brought, a pair of jeans and a red halter, she nearly ran into Owen, who was headed toward the bathroom.

"Oops, sorry," she said, and took a step back.

Owen gave her a quick up-and-down look that made her want to drag him into the bedroom and take off the clothes she'd just put on. "You're going out?"

"Yeah. Chloe should be here any minute. We decided we needed a girls' night."

"Didn't you all just have lunch the other day?"

She smiled at him. "Not the same thing. I'm in the mood to have some fun."

The sound of a car outside drew her attention. "There's Chloe. See ya later." As she went to pass Owen, he reached out and placed his hand against her naked arm.

He met her eyes and looked as though he was about to say something. She wondered if he wanted to ask her to stay but was holding it in because he thought he should. Well, it didn't matter. She wasn't going to get so wrapped up in a man again that she couldn't see herself or what was right in front of her.

"Be careful," he finally said.

Linnea lifted her hand and patted his cheek. "Don't worry. I won't do anything you wouldn't do." She had no idea where that sass had come from, but she kind of liked it and the feeling of freedom and control it gave her, as though she was beginning to emerge from the dark place she'd fallen into when she found out about Michael's lies of omission.

As she walked toward the front door, she heard Owen say something softly that sounded like "That's what I'm afraid of."

When she and Chloe reached the music hall, their friends had already staked a claim on a table in the corner. They made their way through the crowd to join Keri, India, Skyler, Elissa and two women Linnea didn't know.

"Hey," Keri said, catching Linnea's attention. "I convinced my sisters-in-law to join us. Linnea, this is Grace and Brooke."

After a round of hellos, Chloe and Linnea slid into the two chairs that their friends had been saving for them.

"Perfect timing," Chloe said as a huge platter of hot wings and cheese fries was delivered to the table.

"I hear this bunch is trying to talk you into

becoming the newest citizen of Blue Falls," Grace said.

"Yes. It's definitely tempting."

"Well, take it from two gals who uprooted and moved here," she said, gesturing between herself and Brooke. "It's a great place to live."

"The abundance of hot cowboys doesn't hurt, either," Elissa said with a grin before she chomped down on a fry.

Skyler shifted her attention to her friend. "Honestly, you're the only one here who didn't marry a cowboy."

"Pete still looks good in jeans, boots and a Stetson. And out of them, too." Elissa wiggled her eyebrows, drawing laughter from everyone at the table.

Even Linnea laughed, too, determined to have a good time tonight. And as she talked with the other women at the table, she felt as if she belonged. While she had good friends in Dallas, this felt different, as if she'd come home even though she'd never lived in Blue Falls, had never even had the urge to live in some romanticized small town.

"This looks like the place to be."

They all looked to where a tall, lanky cowboy stood next to the table.

"I find myself with an impossible question to answer," he said. "Which of you pretty ladies should I ask to dance?"

Elissa leaned forward. "Well, that's an easy answer. The only one who isn't married." She pointed at Linnea.

The cowboy smiled and extended his hand. "What about it?"

For a moment, Linnea hesitated, wondering if she was really ready to do this. But the urging of her friends propelled her to her feet. She took the man's hand and allowed him to accompany her to the dance floor. By the time he'd led her around the floor a couple of times, he had her laughing. Even so, a part of her kept remembering when it had been Owen dancing with her.

The memory was still there in the front of her mind when she glanced toward the bar and saw him standing next to his brother watching her. The moment their eyes met, he turned his back to her. A sharp pang pierced her chest. Irritation that it even mattered how Owen Brody acted toward her quickly followed, and she threw herself into another dance with her handsome dance partner, and then two more songs with another man who cut in. She laughed when she heard hoots of encouragement from the corner table.

She would not let it bother her that Owen had vacated the bar in favor of talking to a pretty brunette in a different corner of the building. Nor the fact that he was leaning so close to the woman that they had to be breathing the same air.

When the song ended, she aimed to take

a break and rejoin the girls. But she felt yet someone else take her hand. Okay, maybe another dance would take her mind off Owen. She turned and gasped when she came face-to-face with Michael. And the look in his eyes froze her more thoroughly than an ice storm sweeping across Texas.

Chapter Eight

Owen tried to pay attention to what Sarah Finch was saying, but his mind was elsewhere. Like out in the middle of the dance floor where Linnea was dancing with anyone who asked. He should have stayed at home. Linnea would be safe in a crowd this size. But it wasn't just concern for her safety that had brought him to town, was it? No, he hadn't been able to stop thinking about her proposition the night before. He'd had to use that "other way of dealing with desire" before he was able to fall asleep. And all day, while Garrett and his dad had been out taking care of the herd, it had been impossible to stop thinking about marching into the house and taking her up on her offer, consequences be damned.

No matter how hard he tried, he couldn't figure out why his feelings toward Linnea had changed. After all the years he'd known her, spent time with her, why was he suddenly thinking about stripping her naked and licking her up one side and down the other?

Movement from the opposite corner drew his attention. Chloe had shot to her feet and was striding toward the dance floor with a determined look on her face. A wave of cold went through him as he jerked his attention to the crowd of dancers. His heart stuttered when he couldn't find Linnea, but then a couple danced out of the way and he saw Michael pulling Linnea close.

Without a word to Sarah, he strode toward the dance floor, bumping into several people along the way. Owen had sworn to himself that if that bastard ever touched Linnea again, he was going to make good on his promise of making Michael wish he'd never crossed paths with him.

"Owen," Chloe said when he got close to her.

"I see him." He didn't stop walking.

Owen gave Michael no warning this time, just pushed him away from Linnea so hard that he stumbled into another guy. Released so suddenly, Linnea lost her footing, as well, but Owen reached out to steady her without taking his eyes off Michael.

"I told you to leave her alone."

Michael took a slow, deliberate step toward them. "We were just talking. She hasn't given me a chance to explain."

"There's nothing to explain," Linnea said. "You're married. Go home to your wife, and leave me alone."

"You heard the lady." Owen put himself between Linnea and her ex.

Michael leveled a look so cold and calculating at him that Owen wanted to slug him just for existing. Then he shifted his gaze to Linnea. "You say I can't possibly love you, but I guess I could say the same about you if you're already spreading your legs for some common cowboy."

Rage flooded Owen, not at the insult toward him but for how the bastard was treating Linnea. She deserved so much better than that uppity piece of trash. The rage hit a boiling point, and Owen slugged Michael so hard that the other man flew off his feet before landing on his back in the middle of the dance floor.

Gasps and sounds of alarm came from the crowd as they all took several collective steps back. But Owen wasn't done. One punch wasn't nearly enough for what Michael had done, for the insults he'd spewed. Owen stalked toward Michael with every intention of kicking him while he was down. When someone caught hold of his arms from behind, he fought to free himself.

"Stop," Garrett said with that authoritative tone of an older brother.

"Let me go."

"No." Garrett's fingers bit into Owen's arms even harder. "Not here."

Owen still struggled until Linnea placed herself in front of him and laid her palm against his chest. She met his gaze with a pleading look.

"Thank you, but that's enough."

It wasn't nearly enough, but a sliver of common sense found its way through, making him realize that the middle of the Blue Falls Music Hall wasn't the ideal place to dole out some much-needed punishment. As if to put an exclamation point on that fact, Simon Teague stepped into the middle of things just as Michael got to his feet.

"You're going to pay for that," Michael spat past his bloody lip.

Simon held out a hand toward both of them. "That's enough out of both of you. Now, what the devil is going on?"

Keri walked up next to her husband along with Chloe. "That's Linnea's ex," Keri said.

"And she'd already told him to stay away from her," Chloe added.

Simon probably knew all the details from Keri, but he still looked at Linnea. "Is that true?"

Linnea didn't even acknowledge Michael's presence as she nodded.

Simon turned toward Michael. "Then I suggest you vacate the premises."

"He's the one who punched me. I was just talking to my fiancée."

This time, Linnea did look at Michael. Even though he wasn't touching her, Owen could feel the anger radiating off her. "I am not your fiancée. You're married."

"Not for long."

"Ask me how much I don't care."

Owen didn't like the anger he saw on Michael's face as he slowly turned and headed toward the door. It was an expression that promised payback. Owen touched Linnea's shoulder, letting her know he was there and would do whatever it took to protect her as they watched Simon follow Michael out of the building.

"You want to go back to the house?"

Linnea took a deep breath and stood up straighter. "No. I came out to have fun, and that's exactly what I intend to do."

As if on cue, the music started again. Owen didn't want to release her, but he did. He'd protect her however he could, but the last thing she needed was to get tangled up with another guy who couldn't give her what she deserved.

Thankfully, the rest of her girls' night crew surrounded her, and he drifted back to the bar. He caught Linnea's eyes, and the smile she gave him nearly made him have to hide his lower half behind the bar for a while. Sarah made her way back to him. Though he'd much rather be spending time with Linnea, he'd told her, and tried to tell himself, that it was a bad idea. So it wasn't fair to ignore Sarah, who was nice enough and pretty.

But she didn't get his blood pumping the way Linnea did.

Trying to shove thoughts of Linnea out of his head, he escorted Sarah to the dance floor.

"So, what was up with that guy you punched?"

"He's been harassing my sister's best friend."

Sarah looked up at him with an expression that said she knew more was going on. If he was being that obvious, he really needed to rein in his feelings. If he wasn't willing to act on them, he had to find a way to banish them.

But as he and Garrett followed Chloe and Linnea back to the ranch later, he still felt as if an electric current were joyriding on the blood pumping through his body.

"What's with you?" Garrett asked from the driver's seat.

"Nothing."

"Right. So how do you explain the fidgeting? This have to do with Linnea?"

Before he could catch himself, Owen jerked his gaze to his brother. He realized his mistake when Garrett shook his head slowly.

"Don't go down that road. Chloe will have your hide."

"I don't know what you're talking about."

Garrett snorted. "I'm a man, too. I know what it looks like when a guy's amped up over a woman."

It was Owen's turn to make a sound of disbelief. "Really? When was the last time you even went out with a woman?"

"Kind of hard to find someone you haven't already dated."

Okay, that stung. And even considering how

much he dated around, it was a gross exaggeration. "Sounds like an excuse to me."

"And this conversation isn't about me. I've seen how you've been looking at Lin, and it's not a good idea."

"You think I don't know that?" And honestly, it ticked him off that his past decisions were coming back to haunt him right when he wished they didn't exist at all.

When they reached the ranch, he hopped out of the truck almost before it stopped moving and headed straight for the barn. The way he was feeling right now, one part angry and one part horny as a deer with a full rack, he couldn't even be in the house with Linnea. As he stalked into the barn, he wished he was the sort of guy who had a punching bag hanging from the roof, because he could sure use a way to burn off some of the agitation and need vibrating within him.

Instead, he settled for checking on the horses

and some planning for his training business. No matter what he did, however, the buzzing inside him didn't go away. If he didn't think it might put her in danger, he'd wish Linnea would go back to Dallas so he wouldn't be tempted by her all the time.

He sank onto a pile of hay bales stacked against the small room that served as office, tack storage and bunk room all in one. Wyatt had spent some time living in the space before he and Chloe were married. Owen was beginning to think he'd be better off there than under the same roof as Linnea, but then he'd have to explain to his dad why he was sleeping in the barn when he had a perfectly good bed in the house.

Owen was so lost in his thoughts that he didn't hear the footsteps approaching until someone walked into the end of the barn. He leaped to his feet, ready to give Michael a real thrashing he wouldn't forget any time soon. But it wasn't Linnea's ex but rather the woman herself.

"You okay?" he asked.

"Yeah, but I can't seem to fall asleep."

He knew he should keep his distance from her, but as she approached, it was as if the bottom of his boots had adhered to the ground beneath his feet. As she got near, he'd swear he could smell the same flowery scent he had when he'd stood next to her at the music hall earlier.

Linnea stopped an arm's length in front of him. "Thank you for earlier."

"I'm surprised you approve of me punching him."

"Truth is if you hadn't, I might have. And I'm guessing your fist got the point across better."

He lifted an eyebrow.

"That surprises you?"

"Yeah. You don't seem like the type to go around punching people."

"I don't typically have a reason to."

"Do you think you should take out a restraining order against him?"

Linnea took another step toward Owen, sending his pulse into overdrive. "I don't want to talk about Michael."

"Okay." Damn if his voice didn't sound strangled.

Another step brought her so close it took all his effort not to pull her into his arms. He tried to remind himself of all the reasons getting involved with her was a really bad idea, but it proved harder than it should be.

"Lin, don't."

She lifted her fingers to his lips. "Stop telling me why we shouldn't satisfy the yearning we're both feeling. I'm not asking for commitment. I just want to be held, to feel good." She looked deeply into his eyes. "To satisfy my curiosity."

"Damn it, woman, you're trying to kill me."

Linnea ran her hand up his chest. "That's not what I'm trying to do, and you know it."

A man only had so much willpower. With a growl of pure animal need, he wrapped his arms around her and pulled her close. As the last voice telling him to stop was silenced, he captured her mouth with his.

LINNEA WOULD SWEAR she'd been swept up in a wildfire as Owen's mouth took possession of hers. Somehow, beyond the ecstasy of his kisses, she noticed the hard length of him pressing against her stomach. It caused a rush of fresh warmth to flow through her. Her fingers dug into the flexing muscles of his back as he lifted her and sat her atop a stack of hay bales. When he stepped in between her legs, an intense yearning started pulsing in her center.

"Make love to me, Owen," she breathed against his lips.

"Someone might come out here."

"Garrett and your dad already went to bed."

Owen made a sound low in his throat, as if he were trying to be good but failing against her determination to feel every inch of him.

She was tired of simply daydreaming about making love to him, sick of feeling rejected and adrift, frustrated by his need to be noble where she was concerned.

Owen seemed to lose the battle with himself as he dipped his mouth to her neck and his hands made their way below her shirt. Her heart thudded faster as his calloused palms skimmed over her breasts on their way to her back to unclasp her bra. When the bra fell open, his hands returned to her naked breasts. She threw her head back as his talented mouth took a tour up to her ear, then down and around her neck. In the next moment, he pulled the shirt over her head and tossed it aside. The bra joined it in the next breath.

His gaze met hers for a moment, and she

saw such fire there that her body throbbed with need. She ran her hand through his hair and pulled him down to her mouth for another mind-melting kiss.

"You taste so good," he said, his breathing rough.

It felt so wonderful, so empowering to have this effect on a man like Owen, a man so full of testosterone that it oozed from his pores.

Again, his mouth started exploring. When that wet heat settled over one of her breasts, she nearly bucked off the hay bale. His tongue joined the party, and she thought she might climax before she got the rest of her clothes off.

Owen pulled back just enough to catch her gaze. "You like that, huh?"

"I'd think that much was obvious."

Even his chuckle made her hot for him, wanting to feel more of the man.

"Take off your shirt," she said.

Owen didn't immediately comply, instead setting his mouth to work on her other breast. Just when she thought she might explode, he stepped away with a mischievous grin and started to unbutton his shirt slowly, drawing out her desire to see what lay beneath that cotton fabric.

When he finally finished with the last button and let his shirt hang open, her breath caught at the tempting flesh. She grabbed the open panels of the shirt and tugged him toward her, dragging the shirt down his arms and letting it fall to the floor.

"Impatient, Miss Holland?"

Instead of answering with words, she brought her mouth to those finely toned pectorals and licked one of his nipples. She looked at him and grinned. "Does that answer your question?"

She didn't know where the saucy, adventurous side of her was coming from, but it was thrilling. She'd never been this way with Michael, and now she wondered if somewhere down deep inside herself, some part of her had known it wasn't right. But at the moment she wasn't looking for right, just right now.

Owen pressed against her, and she didn't even mind the feel of the rough planks of the wall against her back. The delicious feel of flesh on flesh erased everything else around them. He kissed her as if she were his lifeblood, and her hands drifted down until they found their way below the top of his jeans. Telling herself that for tonight she wasn't going to allow herself to think, only feel, she started working his belt free as he ravaged her mouth. Again, he captured a breast and tongued her until she was in danger of exploding. She unzipped his jeans and filled her hand with the thickness straining to break free.

Owen bucked against her hand and brought his mouth to her ear. "Are you sure about this?"

She nipped his ear with her teeth. "Stop talking and take me."

After he grabbed their discarded clothes so

no one would happen upon them, his hands went to her hips. He lifted her off the hay bale and into his arms. With her legs circling him, he carried her into the small room off the main part of the barn. When he set her on her feet, they wasted no time shucking the rest of their clothing. But when she stood in front of him completely naked, he looked at her with such a combination of reverence and hunger that every inch of her skin tingled.

He skimmed his hand lightly over her cheek. "Are you sure about this?"

"Positive." At his look of concern, she ran her thumb over his lips. "I don't expect anything beyond tonight, but I do want this."

He kissed her again, and it didn't take long for the demanding hunger to come back. When he guided her to the cot covered with a patch-work quilt, she took a moment to appreciate the beauty of his body. The muscles that came from hard work were covered with taut flesh that she didn't think she'd ever be able to forget.

When she stretched alongside him, draping her leg over his, it was the best feeling she'd had in a very long time. They kissed some more, but it didn't take long for the heat to build back to the boiling point. Owen reached over and took his wallet out of his jeans, retrieved a condom and sheathed himself. She told herself not to think about why he had that condom at the ready, to just be thankful that he did. Because she wanted Owen Brody inside her. With that in mind, she rolled atop him and rubbed herself against the long, hard length of him.

Owen's hands gripped her hips as she teased him until he growled again. She loved that sound, the way it vibrated something inside her. Not able to wait any longer, she lifted herself and slowly took him in. Owen closed his eyes and stilled. She watched as his chest moved with his breaths. Wanting to taste that flesh again, she bent forward and licked him like he was an ice-cream cone.

When she bit his nipple, he bucked inside her. It sent a jolt of undiluted desire through her body, and she rocked against him, taking him in as far as she could. That was all it took to shatter any semblance of self-control either of them had. Owen's hands tightened on her hips as she slid back, then impaled herself on him again.

She lost herself in the increasing pace of their lovemaking, the thundering of her heart, the incredible feel of Owen's powerful body as he rolled her onto her back and appeared to be as swept up by the sensations as she was. The need for release built inside her, causing her to close her eyes, throw back her head and bow her body up against his. Her climax hit her in a shuddering wave, and it seemed to trigger Owen's, as well. Owen helped sustain that awesome feeling until they were both totally spent and then he collapsed beside her, drawing her close to his side.

Her heart continued to hammer in her chest for several moments, and when the reverberation of it lessened in her ears, she could hear Owen's ragged breath, as if his lungs were having trouble remembering how to function normally. That sound, the knowledge that she'd done that to him, made her smile.

"You look happy." He sounded surprised, which in turn surprised her.

She slid her head on the thin pillow enough that she could look into his eyes. "Shouldn't I be?"

He lifted his hand to her cheek, then smoothed some of her tousled hair away from her face. "It's just nice to see."

Maybe he didn't realize it, but there was enough tenderness in his words and his expression that it sent a jolt of fear through her. She could not fall for Owen Brody. She wouldn't let herself. Down that road only lay more heart-ache, and she'd had enough of that for a lifetime. Plus, it was probably just the rush of endorphins playing havoc with her brain. After all, what kind of sense did it make to even think about falling for someone so quickly after she'd been about to pledge her life to another? She needed to focus on enjoying what was between her and Owen for what it was, satisfying physical need, and nothing more.

She ran her hand up over his chest and smiled. "I would think you'd be used to seeing this look on a woman's face."

"I don't sleep around as much as people think."

"Maybe you help perpetuate that belief by not getting serious with anyone."

The light in his eyes dimmed, and Linnea wished she could take back those words even though she had no idea why they'd bothered him.

"Maybe." He rolled onto his back and stared at the rough board ceiling.

She propped herself up on her elbow and looked down at him. "Did I say something wrong?"

Owen met her eyes. "Nah."

"Now, why don't I believe you?"

He smiled a little. "You have a suspicious nature?"

"If only that were true. If not for Michael's wife showing up to tell me the truth, I wouldn't be here right now. I'd be hours away from getting married."

His forehead scrunched before realization lit in his eyes. "Your wedding was supposed to be tomorrow."

"Yeah. But instead of being at my rehearsal dinner, I just had some mind-blowing sex."

His mouth curled into a satisfied grin. "That right?"

She skimmed her hand across his flat stomach. "And I wouldn't be opposed to having more." When she cupped him, his hips lifted to press against her.

"And I'm more than happy to oblige."

She giggled when he wrapped his arms around her and rolled atop her again.

After they made love a second time, they curled together and fell asleep. It was sometime in the middle of the night when she woke and realized she needed to go back to the house if they both didn't want to do some explaining in the morning. She dressed as quietly as she could so she wouldn't disturb him. Before she headed for the door, she paused to watch him sleep. His incredibly sexy body made her own hum so much that she wanted to crawl back into bed and wake him up for round three. But she needed to walk away while this was still just them scratching an itch.

Still, she watched him a few moments longer, remembering how incredible he'd made her feel and wondering what memory she had dragged up that he hadn't shared. Had he cared for someone more than anyone had ever expected? A sliver of jealousy hit her, telling her that she shouldn't linger any longer.

She froze when the door squeaked, but Owen didn't move. He appeared to be so deep in sleep that it would take the ringing of a gong right next to his ear to wake him. She smiled at that as she eased out into the main alley of the barn. When she reached the entrance, she paused. Apprehension rose, threatening to choke her, as she looked out into the deep darkness of the night. What seemed like a short distance between the barn and the house during the day felt as if it had expanded tenfold when cloaked in shadows and possible hiding spaces for Michael. She didn't think he'd show up at the ranch again, especially not after the altercation at the music hall earlier, but she wouldn't swear to it. It made her sick to think she'd almost said "I do" to a man she hadn't known at all.

She tried not to think about it as she hurried toward the house, her heart beating fast. She didn't want to dwell on her mistake and the even bigger one she would have made if Danielle had not shown up when she had. When she slipped into the house as quietly as she could, she wondered about Danielle and how she was doing. She hoped Michael's wife divorced him and took him for all he was worth. She normally didn't like vengeful divorce settlements, but Michael had taken the cheating spouse to a whole new level.

She shoved thoughts of Michael from her mind as she eased down the hall, holding her breath until she was safely inside the guest room. After changing into her pajamas and getting into bed, she couldn't stop thinking about Owen, naked and asleep out in the barn. When she closed her eyes, she could still feel his hands on her body, smell his scent on her skin. She'd intended the sex to be a one-time thing, but as she lay there in the dark, she realized that she wanted him even more than she had before he'd relented and taken her to bed.

That, more than anything else, told her it was time to put some distance between her and Owen Brody.

Chapter Nine

What had he done? That was the question that kept playing on repeat in Owen's head as he stared at himself in the mirror the next morning. He'd woken barely early enough to make it back into the house before his dad and Garrett woke up. After the shower and shave had finished waking him up, he still couldn't believe he'd given in to his body's cravings the night before and taken Linnea to bed. What kind of man did that to a woman who'd just been through what she had?

But she'd seemed to enjoy their time together every bit as much as he had.

That didn't matter. She was in a bad spot right now, and he should have been the stronger party. But damn if he hadn't loved the feel of her skin next to his, her feminine scent, and seeing her come alive as he'd made love to her. He started to harden just thinking about it, and he had to grip the edge of the sink to keep from walking straight to her room and sliding into bed with her.

"Damn it." They'd been lucky not to be caught the night before. He sure as hell wasn't going to have sex with her in the house when his dad and brother were within earshot.

A knock sounded at the door. "You talking to yourself in there?" Garrett's voice sounded amused.

Owen ignored his brother as he pulled on his jeans and opened the door.

"Don't you look cheerful this morning?" Garrett said as Owen walked past him.

When Owen flipped him the bird, Garrett just

chuckled before going into the bathroom. As Owen passed the guest room door, it opened to reveal Linnea standing there in a pair of skimpy summer pajamas consisting of shorts and a top with spaghetti straps. He didn't know why that sight made him go rock hard when he'd seen her completely naked the night before, but it did. Before he could corral enough brain cells to continue on down the hall, Linnea reached out and grabbed one of his belt loops to pull him inside the bedroom. As he was too surprised to respond appropriately, the next thing he knew she was closing the bedroom door and pressing her body next to his.

She smiled up at him. "Good morning."

He gripped her shoulders and pushed her away. "What are you doing?"

She flinched at his question, and her smile dimmed. He wanted to curse himself for causing that reaction.

"I'm sorry. I thought you had a good time last night."

Though he knew he should keep his hands to himself, he lifted one to one of her bare shoulders. "I did, but you said it was a one-time thing."

"No, I said it was a no-strings-attached fling. I didn't say anything about it being just last night."

He shook his head. "This isn't a good idea, Lin. You're going to wake up one morning and regret it."

"No, I won't."

He was surprised by how much he wanted to believe her, and that in itself was dangerous. He did not form those types of attachments, at least not anymore. And especially not with his sister's best friend. To do so had disaster written all over it.

"I'm not what you're looking for."

"How about you let me decide what I want?"

He had to get out of this room before she wore him down. "I've got work to do." Hoping that no one saw him, he jerked the door open and fled to his own room.

Unwilling to let himself stay near temptation, he volunteered to take Cletus to the vet, since he'd been acting under the weather. He didn't know who was going to stay around the ranch to keep an eye out for any unwanted reappearances by Michael, but it wasn't going to be him. Because for some reason, Linnea made all common sense take a hike.

While Dr. Franklin, the vet, checked on Cletus, Owen kept himself busy getting a few supplies from the hardware store, doing the grocery shopping and finally stopping by the Primrose for some lunch.

"Hey, baby brother," Chloe said with a wave from where she was sitting at a table with Elissa and her aunt Verona. When he sank onto the one empty chair at the table, Chloe asked, "Who's with Linnea?"

He shrugged. "Either Dad or Garrett. I had to bring Cletus to the vet, run a few errands."

"How is Linnea doing?" Verona asked. "Such a sad thing to happen to such a sweet girl."

"Pretty well, considering," Chloe said. "I'm thinking about throwing a little surprise party for her birthday. It's this weekend."

"That's a great idea," Elissa said. "Get her mind off that ass she was engaged to."

"Invite some eligible bachelors."

Elissa looked at her aunt as if she'd lost her mind. "Really? I'd think the last thing she'd want anything to do with right now is a man."

"Just because she had one bad experience doesn't mean the right guy for her isn't out there somewhere. Maybe even here in Blue Falls."

"Lord," Elissa said with a roll of her eyes. "Single men are going to become an endangered species around here soon with the way you're trying to pair everyone up."

"I don't see you complaining about how it turned out for you."

"And I wasn't coming off the mother of all breakups, either."

Owen thought his head was going to explode from all the chatter. Why had he sat down?

"I still maintain that her meeting the right guy will be the cure for what ails her."

When Verona glanced at Owen, that was the last straw.

"I've got to go pick up Cletus." He thought he saw a knowing smile on Verona's mouth, but he pretended he'd seen nothing of the sort.

"Don't tell Linnea about the party," Chloe said as he stood.

"I understand the word *surprise*, you know."

Before Verona figured out how to rope him into walking down the aisle, Owen hurried toward the door. He was outside with his stomach growling before he remembered why he'd gone into the Primrose in the first place.

LINNEA LOOKED UP from her laptop when she heard Owen's truck slow at the turn into the driveway. He'd spent the better part of the day away from the ranch, and while she had no doubt he actually was doing everything Garrett had claimed, she also knew it was a good excuse to avoid her.

Fine. If he didn't want to share any more intimacies with her, she'd respect that. Though a part of her was convinced that he wanted a repeat of the previous night as much as she did. But she wasn't going to push it.

So when he parked, she didn't even look his way. Instead, she kept going over the financial reports Katrina had sent her. Linnea's personal life might be a giant mess, but at least her business was doing really well. She paused to daydream about how she could make the store space in Blue Falls into something just as exciting as her Dallas shop.

She looked up as Owen lifted Cletus from the front seat of the truck and set him gently on the ground. Roscoe jumped up and waddled down the steps, then crossed the yard to sniff Cletus.

Linnea couldn't help but smile. "I think Roscoe missed his buddy. He's been lying here sighing all day."

Owen crossed his arms as he watched the doggie reunion. "These two don't know what to do without each other. Silly dogs."

"I think they're adorable."

Owen squatted and petted both the dogs. "Yeah. Guess we wouldn't know what to do without them, either." He finally looked up at her then. "Do you have pets?"

"No, never have. Mom's allergic to cats, and she always said dogs were too much work. I think that's why I always liked coming out here with Chloe. I like animals and have never had any."

He grinned. "Just not horses."

"Let's just say I admire them from afar."

Were it not for the fact that she knew what every inch of Owen's body looked like now, their conversation would feel almost like old times, before they'd given in to their mutual attraction. But she'd never be able to look at him the same way again.

Something changed about the way he was looking at her, and she wondered if he was thinking about them making love. Did he want to indulge again as much as she wanted to? She nearly asked him before she remembered her promise to herself to respect his wishes.

"Well, I better get to work," he said as he stood.

"Training horses today or riding the range?"

"Guess I better ride out, since they're short-handed today." He looked around. "Who stayed behind?"

"Nobody. I told them I'd be fine."

When he looked upset that she'd been left alone, she tried not to read too much into it. "I can't have a bodyguard all the time. I won't have one when I go home."

"At home, you'll be within yelling distance of neighbors if you need help."

"Michael may be upset and trying to get me to come back to him, but he won't do something too drastic."

Owen pinned her with an intense gaze. "Are you sure about that?"

She opened her mouth to respond but found she couldn't swear to being sure. After all, she would never have believed Michael would lie to her in such a brutal way, and yet he did.

Without saying anything else, Owen shook his head and stalked off toward the barn. Not in the mood to work anymore, she took her computer inside. But being in the house felt confining, so she walked out to the corral to watch Owen work with one of the horses he was training for barrel racing. As she leaned against the fence, it struck her anew how incredibly good Owen looked astride a horse, as though it was where he was meant to be. She could get used to seeing that every day.

That thought startled her enough that she backed away from the fence without consciously thinking about doing so. She could not let herself get emotionally attached to Owen. Physical release was one thing, and maybe he was right that they shouldn't repeat that performance. After what she'd been through with Michael, this time needed to be for healing, not jumping right into another relationship. She laughed a little under her breath at that. As if Owen would even think about a serious relationship.

Still, the thought of what they'd done in the

barn caused heat to rise in her face. She placed her palms against her flushed cheeks.

Owen rode the horse close to the fence and stopped. "You okay?"

"Yeah, just a little hot. I think I'll go in and get something to drink. You want anything?"

"Nah, I'm good."

As she walked back to the house, she didn't look over her shoulder even though she felt as if Owen was watching her. If she was being honest with herself, she liked the idea of him watching her and liking what he saw. But as she climbed the front steps, she told herself that was because she needed some bolstering to her ego, nothing more.

She'd just poured a glass of lemonade when Owen stepped through the back door into the kitchen.

"I changed my mind," he said.

Her heart rate started galloping like a wild horse. "Oh?"

He nodded toward the glass in her hand. "A cold drink sounds good after all."

"Oh."

He cocked his head a bit to the side. "Are you sure you're okay?"

"Yeah, fine." If by fine, she meant every nerve ending in her body was sizzling as if some switch had been turned on inside her.

She turned and poured another glass of lemonade and extended it to Owen. When he took it and their fingers brushed against each other, he seemed to linger, drawing out the contact. Was he changing his mind about other things, as well? She didn't want to play a guessing game, so she looked up at him.

"I need to know something," she said.

"Okay."

"Do you want to continue what we started last night? Because, if not, I'll pack up and head back to Dallas. I don't want to make you uncomfortable."

"You don't make me uncomfortable, Lin." He paused as he held her gaze. "At least not in the way you're thinking."

"What's that supposed to mean?"

Owen slowly set his glass on the table, then took hers and placed it beside his. "I'm really uncomfortable right now, and there's only one way to cure it." When he looked back at her, desire had burst to life in his eyes.

"I thought you said this was a bad idea."

"It probably is."

But in the next moment, he pulled her close and kissed her so deeply her own desire shot up at least a thousand degrees. When his hands slipped under her shirt and up over her breasts, she gasped.

"You like that?"

Owen's wicked grin demanded payback, so she rubbed her hand along the front of his jeans that were doing little to hide the rigid length of him. "I could ask the same thing."

Owen growled deep in his throat and picked her up. She wrapped her legs around his back as he sat her on the countertop and ripped off her shirt and bra. Then his mouth captured her right breast as if she was the most delectable dish in the world and he was determined to taste his fill.

The feel of his tongue lapping at her was nearly enough to make her reach climax all on its own. But somehow a sliver of sound reached through the haze and caused her to freeze. "Owen." At first he didn't respond, not until she pushed back on his shoulders. "Listen."

The sound of approaching footsteps made Linnea squeak as she jumped off the counter and grabbed her shirt and bra. With no time to put them on, she raced for the guest bedroom, barely reaching it before she heard the back door open and then muffled voices. She clutched her shirt and bra to her chest as she leaned back against the door, her heart beating so hard she could hear it reverberating against her eardrums.

That had been close. Way too close.

OWEN BARELY HAD time to grab his glass of lemonade before Chloe walked into the house. He leaned his hip against the sink, trying to look way more casual than he felt. Damn, he'd been on the verge of taking Linnea right there in the kitchen without thinking of the potential consequences. What the heck was wrong with him? He'd told himself to stay away, and yet he seemed powerless to do so.

"Hey," Chloe said. "Didn't expect you to be in the house."

He lifted the glass. "Got thirsty."

As she approached him, she put on her doctor face.

"Did you get too hot? You look really flushed."

When she tried to lift the back of her hand to his forehead, he took a step away, irrationally afraid she'd see the truth if she touched him. "I'm okay. Stop being a worrywart."

She rolled her eyes. "You are so stubborn."

"Runs in the family."

She glanced toward the living room. "Where's Lin?"

He shrugged. "Around. Saw her on the porch when I got back."

Chloe's gaze fell on the other glass of lemonade sitting on the table, sweat streaking down the sides. She glanced at him as if wheels inside her head were turning, wheels he needed to stop. But it was as if his brain froze.

"Oh, hey. I thought I heard someone come in." Linnea breezed into the kitchen as if he hadn't just been feasting on her delicious naked skin minutes before. "Had to take a call from Katrina. One of the store's shipments somehow ended up in Butte, Montana."

Linnea didn't make eye contact with him. Probably a good decision. She grabbed her glass of lemonade and looked at Chloe instead. "Shouldn't you be at work?"

"It's my afternoon off. I came to ask you a favor if you're up to it."

"Sure."

"Elissa's cousin just got engaged, and she's almost as clueless about fashion as Elissa is. I was hoping maybe you could meet her Friday and give her some pointers about wedding gowns. But if you're not up to it, I totally understand."

"It's fine. It's my business. I'm not letting Michael steal that from me, too."

Her words were brave and determined, but Owen still saw the layer of hurt Michael had caused. His grip on the glass tightened as he wished he could punch that bastard again. He didn't make a habit of fighting, but it wasn't often he ran into someone who'd done something so wrong to someone he cared about. If there was ever anyone who deserved to be punched in the face, it was Michael Benson.

"Great," Chloe said, then gave Linnea a hug.

Owen held out an arm. "What, no hug for your brother?"

Chloe curled up her nose. "You've been out working in the sun. I'm sure you stink."

"Just for that…" He started for his sister, and she squealed as she made for the front door.

After she'd closed the door behind her, Linnea let out a breath and leaned against one of the kitchen chairs. "That was entirely too close."

Something twisted in Owen's middle. Despite the fact that he'd had the same thought, it bothered him that Linnea would have been embarrassed to be caught with him. He tried to shake off the odd feeling, telling himself it would have bothered her to be caught with anyone that way, especially when she was staying in someone else's home. But a part of him wasn't so hot on the hidden fling anymore, and he wasn't willing to examine why.

He placed his now-empty glass in the sink. "I better get back to work."

He half expected Linnea to try to stop him, but she didn't. As he walked back toward the barn, he hated how much that bothered him, too.

Chapter Ten

Linnea wanted to grab Owen and drag him to the guest bedroom to finish what they'd started before Chloe's arrival. But the fact that she'd been moments away from being found half-naked with her best friend's brother in the middle of the kitchen told her that they needed someplace safer to be together. And she did want to be with him again, as soon as possible. Her body seemed to be buzzing with desire. She honestly didn't recognize herself.

Needing to get away from the ranch for a while or risk marching out to the barn and attacking Owen, she headed for her car. She didn't have a destination in mind, but she ended up at a natural area on the north side of Blue Falls Lake. She'd made sure to watch her rearview mirror on the off chance that Michael had been lurking in town waiting for the opportunity to get her alone again. She shook her head at the paranoia and got out of the car. After consulting a trail map, she headed up the Lakeview Trail.

She might be a city girl, but it felt good to stretch her legs surrounded by Mother Nature, even if the heat was a touch stifling. As she climbed the rocky path, she let her thoughts wander. The responsibilities of her real life called to her, and she knew she'd have to answer that call soon. But she wasn't quite ready, and that wasn't just because she might have to deal with Michael again. There was something blazing between her and Owen, and she hadn't yet gotten enough of it.

When she reached the top of the trail, the

view was spectacular. The sun glinted off the surface of the lake. Boats of various types, including a small paddle wheeler, glided across the water. Skyler's Wildflower Inn sat atop a smaller hill on the opposite side of the lake, and the downtown buildings of Blue Falls were so picturesque in the distance that Linnea fell a little more in love with the place.

Why was she experiencing such a pull toward the town now when she never had before? Sure, she'd always thought it was cute, but now it felt as if a magnet was drawing her with its invisible force. Was it just the need to be in surroundings that didn't remind her of Michael? Maybe it was simply the excitement of something new and different for her business. Or was she letting her feelings toward Owen veer dangerously away from pure physical satisfaction? That couldn't be it, could it? Not so soon after the nuclear meltdown of her relationship with Michael, anyway.

She sank onto a bench and watched the boats on the lake as she tried to sort out her feelings. For the second time that day, the sound of approaching footsteps startled her. But when she spun toward the trail, it was Owen instead of his sister.

"You followed me?"

"Yep." He didn't sound the least bit sorry about it.

"That wasn't necessary. I was careful."

He came over and sat beside her. "Here's the thing. I don't trust that Michael is done harassing you, and I'm not about to give him the opportunity to get you alone. At least not while you're here in my backyard."

Not wanting to think about Michael or the fact that he evidently turned into a different person when he didn't get his way, she smiled at Owen. "Are you sure you didn't just want to finish what we started in the kitchen?"

He laughed a little. "Who are you, and what

have you done with prim and proper Linnea Holland?"

"Are you saying I'm normally a bore?"

Owen shifted toward her. "No. But until recently you wouldn't have given anyone like me a second look."

"Like you?"

"Rough around the edges, not refined."

"I tried refined, and he turned out to be a giant horse's ass."

Owen nodded. "True. That still doesn't explain me."

She ran her hand up his thigh, drawing a sound from him that set her blood to pumping. "You mean besides the fact that you're sexy as hell?"

He seemed to forcibly pull himself up from the fog of sexual desire to give her a serious look. "Yeah."

Was he worried about being used? She retrieved her hand and placed it in her lap. "I'm sorry. I didn't mean to be pushy."

Owen captured her hand between his. "I'm not upset. Just curious, I guess."

When she looked over at him, he wore an expression she'd never seen on his face before, one that showed more vulnerability than she'd realized he harbored.

"You really don't know what a good person you are, do you?"

He looked startled by her question. "It's not the first thought that pops into people's heads when they think of me."

"Then they're blind."

"I'm not as nice as you think I am."

"All I know is that you've been kind and caring toward me, and that's how I see you act toward most people. Honestly, I don't know why some lucky girl hasn't snapped you up yet."

He barked out a laugh at that.

"What's so funny about that?"

"I don't give them the chance to even try. Remember, I'm a bed hopper."

"You said that wasn't true."

"People think lots of things that aren't true."

She narrowed her gaze at him. "You want people to think that about you. Why?"

He sighed. "Because getting close to people isn't worth the risk."

Part of her wanted to agree with him, but there was enough of her true self left that she couldn't. "You say that when you see how happy Chloe is with Wyatt?"

"She got lucky. Not everyone does."

She watched him as he stared out toward the lake. "Did someone hurt you?"

"We've all been hurt by someone at some point."

She could tell by his answer that he didn't want to talk about the person who'd been his someone. As she tried to imagine him in a serious relationship, it wasn't as hard as it'd once been. There were deeper layers to Owen, ones he did his best to hide. But now wasn't the time to press him for details. It wasn't her right to ask for that information, anyway. After all, they were nothing more than friends with benefits, right? She tried to ignore how that thought didn't sit comfortably in her mind.

"You hungry?" Owen's question was out of the blue, but at the mention of food she realized she was indeed hungry.

"Yeah, actually."

"Let's go get some pizza." He stood and extended his hand.

The moment Linnea placed her hand in his, the electricity that had been sparking between them earlier returned.

"Of course, food isn't all I'm hungry for," she said, feeling her cheeks flush at her honesty.

Owen grinned. "That right?"

Linnea pressed herself against him and looked

up into his eyes. "After the pizza, maybe we can find a good place for dessert."

He ran his fingers through her hair to the back of her head. "I've got to say I like this new Lin."

And then he not only kissed her but kissed her until her knees nearly buckled. He backed her against a cedar tree and ran his hands all over her, igniting a trail of fire in their wake. One of those hands found its way beneath the fabric of her shorts, and when his fingers flicked against her, she pressed toward him, wanting the release his hand promised. When he brought her to the pinnacle, she felt as if she might combust right there on the spot. She gripped his arms, not trusting her shaking legs to hold her weight, and leaned her forehead against his chest.

"You make me lose my mind," she said, her words muffled against his chest.

Owen dropped a kiss atop her head. "I could say the same about you."

The way he held her and the rumble of his voice made something move inside Linnea, but she shoved her awareness of that shift away because she didn't want to acknowledge it. Because she was afraid that despite common sense, her feelings toward Owen were changing.

"We should go," he finally said.

She nodded as she stepped free of his touch to right her clothing and try to get her breathing and spinning thoughts under control. Owen took a few steps away as she turned her back to him. She ambled toward the edge of the lookout point, giving Owen a few moments alone. When he stepped up beside her, she'd swear she could feel waves of heat coming off him that had nothing to do with the warmth of the day.

"It sure is a beautiful view," she said, needing to talk about anything other than the fact that Owen brought out a side of her she'd never thought existed. Oh, it had been there in her fantasies, but she'd never let it out to play in the light of day.

"Yeah. Prettiest place in Texas if you ask me."

"Can't argue with that."

He glanced at her and smiled. "What, you're not missing your skyscrapers and rush-hour traffic?"

"That's not all Dallas is about." But she had to admit that she hadn't missed it as much as she thought she would. And she didn't think that was totally because she now associated that part of her life with Michael and what he'd done.

They stood in silence a few more moments as the sun inched closer to the horizon. An incredible sense of belonging hit Linnea as she scanned the vista before her, followed by the thought that she could be happy in Blue Falls. She knew her feelings might be clouded by what was occurring between her and Owen, but her heart told her it was more. It was as if she was approaching one of life's important forks in the road, and she was going to have to make a decision soon about which one to take.

"Well, I'm officially starving," Owen said, drawing her from her deep thoughts.

"Me, too. I think I could eat an entire pizza all by myself."

As they walked down the trail, Linnea tried not to watch Owen's really nice butt in those well-worn jeans, but they'd only gone a few yards when she gave up. It wasn't as if she hadn't seen what those jeans encased, anyway. And if she had just let him bring her to climax in broad daylight on a public trail, what was a little ogling?

They drove separately to Gia's, the local pizzeria that dished up pizza so good that people drove from different counties to eat there. It was a little slice of Italy in the middle of steak country. By the time Linnea parked a couple of spaces down from Owen, she'd almost gotten her pulse back to normal. But damn if it didn't speed up again as soon as she stepped out of her car to find Owen waiting for her. She gasped before she could stop herself.

Owen chuckled. "Do I make you nervous?"

She snorted, pretending he hadn't just hit the nail on the head like an expert carpenter. Unfortunately, she didn't seem to fool him, since he continued to laugh at her as she pushed past him toward the restaurant.

They weren't seated at their table more than two minutes when Verona Charles walked through the front door. The older woman's eyes brightened when she spotted them. Linnea might not be from Blue Falls, but she'd been there enough to know about Verona and her matchmaking ways. And the way she was eyeing Linnea and Owen and changing course toward them, there was no doubt what was going through her mind.

"Incoming," Linnea said.

"Huh?"

She nodded toward Verona, causing Owen to glance over his shoulder.

"Oh, hell. I know that look."

"Linnea, hon, how are you doing?" Verona was as chipper as a little bird heralding a spring morning.

"Fine. How are you?"

"Great. Glad to see you're out enjoying yourself." She patted Owen on the shoulder. "And with such handsome company."

Linnea only smiled noncommittally and tried not to burst out laughing when she caught Owen's eye roll.

Not one to give up so easily, Verona shifted her focus to Owen. "I'm also happy to see you're making sure Linnea has a good visit to Blue Falls. Maybe you can convince her to stay."

Something flashed across Owen's face that looked a little too much like panic. It shouldn't bother her if what was between them was nothing more than sex, but it did bother her. She couldn't help but wonder if that meant she should think about staying in Blue Falls or if she should race back to Dallas at the first opportunity.

Only when the waitress came to the table to take their order did Verona cease her obvious matchmaking and head to the front counter to pick up a to-go order.

When Owen suggested they get a pizza that had every kind of meat the restaurant had, Linnea swore she could feel her arteries clogging just thinking about it. "How about we go half and half?" And then she ordered her half with mushrooms and pineapple.

"Weirdo," he said as soon as the waitress walked away. "Fruit doesn't go on pizza."

"Whatever, King of Cholesterol."

When Verona picked up her pizza, she shot

them a wide smile and cheery wave as she headed toward the front door.

"I see Verona hasn't changed," Linnea said. "I should bring her to Dallas to drum up business for the shop." Or she might prove useful if Linnea indulged her crazy whim to start a new bridal shop in downtown Blue Falls.

"I swear that woman either has a network of spies or some sort of sophisticated alert system that lets her know whenever two single people get anywhere near each other within the city limits."

Silence settled between them, making Linnea realize that they really didn't have a lot in common. But was that a bad thing? Weren't opposites supposed to attract? That's all it was, pure physical attraction. But that wasn't something she could really indulge in the middle of a pizzeria.

"So, how's the horse training going?"

"Pretty good. If I can make a sale soon, that

would really help. Hard to make a name for yourself when you don't have a track record."

"How are you getting the word out?"

"I mentioned what I was doing to Liam Parrish, India's husband. Wyatt works for him."

"That makes sense with Liam owning the rodeo company that puts on the rodeos here."

Owen nodded. "He does them other places around Texas, too. So maybe he'll hear of somebody looking for a good horse for competition."

"You should go to rodeos yourself and talk to the riders. No one can talk up your work as much as you can."

"Could be a lot of travel that turns up nothing."

She leaned her forearms on the table. "Or it could be what sets you apart from other trainers. Successful businesses usually have to invest before they can start making a profit."

"Easier said than done. I don't have a lot of extra cash lying around."

"I know what you mean. When I signed the papers for my loan to start the shop, I was shaking so hard I could barely write. But I believed in what I wanted to build enough to take that leap of faith."

"And you think I should take a leap like that?"

"Doesn't matter what I think. The question is whether you believe enough to do so."

Their pizza arrived then, and they dived into it as if they'd been without food for a week. When Linnea no longer felt as though her stomach was going to consume itself, she wiped her mouth on her napkin and looked at Owen.

He noticed her watching him. "What?"

She steepled her fingers. "Another thing you could do is develop a website and print some business cards."

"Sounds like more money I haven't made yet."

"Not really. You can do both remarkably

cheap. I could even design them for you, since I did the ones for the shop."

He lowered the piece of pizza he'd just picked up. "You'd do that?"

She smiled. "Sure. It's not like I'm offering to carry you on my back across North America."

But there was something about the look on his face that told her it was a big deal to him. Had no one really ever expressed a belief in him? That made her incredibly sad. A wave of determination to make sure his dream became reality welled up inside her. She might not know anything about horses, but she was reasonably intelligent about how to build a business.

She pointed toward the pizza. "Eat up, horse boy. We've got a website to build."

OWEN WATCHED AS Linnea moved images around the screen of her laptop, each step bringing him closer to actually having a real business.

She pointed toward the screen. "See what I

did there? You can use that to change out information about what horses you have for sale, their traits, backgrounds, et cetera."

"You might as well be typing in Russian."

She looked up at him where he stood leaning over the back of the chair at the kitchen table. All thoughts of the website or training horses flew out of his mind as he stared into her beautiful eyes, as his gaze drifted to those soft lips of hers. He wanted nothing more than to capture her mouth with his, but with his dad and Garrett sitting in the next room watching TV, it wasn't a good idea. If he and Lin showed any sort of hint about what they'd been sharing, everyone would get the wrong idea.

Linnea must have seen his thoughts in his expression, because she suddenly slipped out of the chair then pointed to it.

"Come on. It's not that hard." She pushed him into the chair.

Garrett sauntered into the kitchen. "You know you could train a chimp easier, right?"

Owen gifted him with a rude gesture, but Lin placed her hand on Owen's shoulder and said, "Your brother is smarter than you give him credit for."

Had she just said what he thought she had? When he saw the curious look on Garrett's face, Owen laughed to steer his brother's thoughts away from where Owen feared they were headed.

"And Lin is overly optimistic."

After Garrett deposited his ice-cream bowl in the sink and returned to the living room, Linnea pulled a chair up next to Owen's and sat down.

"Remember what I said earlier. You have to believe in yourself before others will believe in you. So no more negative self-talk."

He gave her a salute, and she responded by

playfully punching him in the arm before pointing toward the computer screen again.

Either she was right and he was smarter than he thought, or she was just a good teacher, because by the time midnight rolled around he was actually able to follow what she was telling him. When she nodded at the computer and told him to enter the information about the horses he was training, he only had to ask her one question. It might not be a big deal to most people, but when he finished the update and she nodded her approval, he felt as if he'd successfully climbed Mount Everest.

Linnea bumped his shoulder with hers. "See, I told you that you could do it."

He turned toward her and cupped her face with his hand. "Thanks to you." Unable to be near her and not kiss her any longer, he lowered his lips to hers.

At first, she responded as though she wanted

the kiss as much as he did, but then she pulled away and looked beyond him.

"Garrett or your dad might come in."

"They're both fast asleep."

"How do you know that?"

"Because I can hear my dad snoring, and Garrett is as predictable as the sunrise." He pulled her close.

She stiffened for a moment, then tilted her face up to his. "I understand why you're so in demand by the local female population."

"That right?"

She smiled, and damn if it didn't make his insides feel funny. An alarm bell started clanging in the back of his mind, but his body was having none of that warning. Instead, he wrapped his arms fully around Linnea and kissed her as he had up at the lookout. She felt so good pressed against him, and his head spun as if he were intoxicated. What was it about her that made him want her every waking moment?

He'd never felt that way, not even with Katy…
No, he wasn't going to think about that disaster when he had a warm and willing woman in his arms. Something about that thought sent such a jolt through him that he stepped away abruptly, causing Linnea to stumble. He automatically reached out to steady her.

"What's wrong?"

He shook his head. "You're right. We shouldn't do this here."

She gave him a sexy smile. "The barn?"

That damn bell got louder and he took another step back. "We better cool it for now."

Her smile faded before his eyes, and part of him wanted to wrap her in his arms again. But another part was telling him that something was changing and he needed to put distance between them.

"I've got to get up early in the morning," he said. "Thanks for the help with the website." Then before his raging erection started thinking for him, he headed out of the kitchen and stalked straight to his bedroom.

Once inside the room that had been his since he was a little boy, he had the strangest urge to lock the door. But it wasn't because he thought Linnea was going to sneak in and have her way with him, because honestly he wouldn't fight that. And that was the crux of the problem. She made him lose his mind so much that he would make love to her when there was every possibility that his dad and Garrett might hear them.

He ran his hand over his face and shucked off his clothes. When he stretched out on his bed, he listened as the floorboards creaked under Linnea's feet as she made her way to the guest room. He thought back over the moment that had sent him backing away from her. It was the thought about having a warm and willing woman in his arms. How many times had he had exactly that and it had been enough? But he'd realized with Linnea, it was more than that. And it freaked him out. Experience had shown him that when you cared too much for someone, fate was waiting right around the corner to take her away from you. Linnea had already been through enough. She didn't need to be collateral damage from his caring too much for her.

Chapter Eleven

Since Chloe had taken Friday off from work, she stopped by to pick up Linnea late that afternoon. After they finished meeting with Elissa's cousin, Chloe said they'd drive over to Austin for dinner and to catch the new Ryan Gosling movie.

When they arrived at the bakery, Keri's sister-in-law, Josephina, was the one manning the counter. Unable to resist the sweet smells filling the building, Linnea bought a lemon cookie to munch on while she and Chloe waited on Elissa and Cami. While Chloe placed her order, Linnea sank onto a chair and stared out the window. The longer she stayed in Blue Falls, the more she felt it enveloping her like an old friend. The faces she passed on the street here seemed to be happy, and she suspected that hers reflected that same happiness.

It was a miracle, really, that she could feel that way after the wreck her life had been when she arrived. But Owen, of all people, had changed all that. Her heart expanded at the memories of how he held her as they kissed, how when they made love he seemed every bit as pleased by her satisfaction as his own, the mingled look of surprise and thankfulness he'd given her when she'd helped him set up his website.

But had her morphing feelings shown themselves? Was that why Owen had kept his distance the past couple of days? He'd spent long hours out on the far reaches of the ranch, only working with the horses he was training when his dad or Garrett was around. Another day he'd spent away from the ranch entirely, off to check on another horse somewhere south of San Antonio. Part of her had wanted him to ask her to come along, but he hadn't. So she'd sat at the ranch doodling sketches of how she would set up a shop in the store space in Blue Falls if she was crazy enough to make that leap and running figures to see if it was even remotely in her financial ballpark.

Chloe snapped her fingers near Linnea's face, drawing her attention.

"Huh?"

Chloe laughed. "You could have been in outer space you were so far away."

"Sorry. Mind was just wandering."

"Anywhere in particular? You've seemed distracted a lot lately."

Linnea shrugged, knowing she needed to stop being so transparent. "Just thinking about what I want the next step in my life to be, I guess."

She realized that at least a part of her liked the idea of taking another step with Owen and not having to hide it. But that hadn't been their deal. It was sex, friendship, nothing more. But that rang hollow somehow, and she wondered if she'd been a fool to think she could be the kind of person who got that intimate with a man without feeling something more than animal desire.

"Are you sure that's all it is?"

Linnea forced a smile she hoped looked genuine. "Yeah. What else would it be?"

Before Chloe had the chance to guess, Elissa and another young woman who favored her walked through the front door. After introductions were made, they spent the next half hour looking through wedding magazines. The familiar buzz of excitement that Linnea feared Michael had damaged beyond repair returned as she talked with Cami about dress styles, designers and accessories.

When Cami seemed to have settled on a general idea of what she wanted, she thanked Linnea for her help.

"I know this isn't really about dresses, but I was wondering if I could ask another favor," Cami said.

"Sure. I'm happy to help any way I can."

"It's about the reception. I'm thinking about having it on the *Lady Fleur*, the paddle-wheel boat out on the lake. Do you have time to come take a look at it with me and tell me what you think?"

Linnea was a little surprised by the request, but what else did she have to do? Owen had been on top of the barn roof with his brother patching a leak when she left the ranch. "Okay."

As she and Chloe followed Elissa and Cami to the dock where the *Lady Fleur* was tied up, Linnea couldn't help but think about all the preparations she'd made for her own wedding reception. Something about her time in Blue Falls made that swanky affair feel as if it belonged in the wedding plans of an entirely different person. A cruise around Blue Falls Lake sounded so much better.

She followed Cami and Elissa on board, glancing out across the stunning beauty of the lake. If she lived here, she'd be near this water all the time. She could totally see herself going for daily walks around the path that circled the lake. She shifted her gaze toward the door in front of her, noticing Cami and Elissa had already disappeared inside. Promising herself a walk around the lake before she left for home, she stepped inside.

"Surprise!"

Linnea jumped and yelped at the same time. It took a moment for her to realize the faces looking back at her were all ones she knew and they all looked really pleased by her reaction.

"Happy birthday!" Chloe's words were followed by cheers from the small crowd.

With her hand against her chest as if that

would slow her pounding heart, she spun toward Elissa and Cami. "This was all a trick to get me here?"

Elissa smiled. "Yes, and it worked beautifully, if I do say so myself."

Linnea turned to Cami. "Are you even getting married?"

Cami shrugged. "Maybe someday. Have to finish college first."

Chloe came over and bumped shoulders with Cami. "She is Elissa's cousin, but she's studying theater at UT. I'd say she's got a pretty good future as an actress, don't you think?"

Linnea scanned the gathering again and noticed the balloon bouquets in the corners and the party hats on the tables. "I can't believe you did all this for me."

Chloe waved away the idea that it was any big deal. "Hon, we'll use any excuse for a party."

Linnea laughed. "You all certainly are sneaky. I had no idea, especially since my birthday isn't for a couple of days." And the fact that she hadn't given it much thought. After all, she'd believed she'd be spending it as a married woman in a tropical paradise.

But her gaze lit on Owen standing with his brother, Wyatt, Liam Parrish and a few other guys, and she thought this was way better than white-sand beaches with the king of liars. Maybe thoughts about her planned wedding reception had felt as if they were for another person because they had been. As crazy as it sounded, she felt as if the days she'd spent here in Blue Falls had changed her. Or perhaps it had just shown her who she really was, down deep.

Her friends showed her to the table where she was to sit. Instead of a party hat, there was a gold paper crown that they insisted she had to wear during the entire party.

She laughed. "Did you raid a kids' party supply store?"

Elissa plopped her party hat on her head.

"They were on sale. Don't say we don't go all out for a friend."

When the boat pulled away from the dock and a lady she didn't recognize started bringing out dishes of barbecue, potato salad and slaw, it hit Linnea how much this little party must be costing her friends.

"You all shouldn't have done this. It's got to be expensive. We could have just gone to Gia's and had pizza."

"But it wouldn't have been a surprise," Skyler said as she stepped up next to Elissa. She gestured first toward Elissa, then India and finally Chloe. "This bunch loves surprises."

Elissa eyed Skyler. "Our surprise for you didn't turn out too bad, now, did it?"

Chloe must have seen Linnea's confused look. "India and Elissa took Skyler tandem skydiving for her birthday last year. It's how she met her husband, Logan."

"There's got to be a better way to meet guys than jumping out of an airplane," Linnea said.

"Exactly!" Skyler looked toward the group of guys. "Though it's true I can't argue with the end result."

When Linnea looked in the same direction, her gaze landed on Owen. Damn, but she wanted him. She knew he tasted better than any birthday cake that might be brought out later.

"Lin?"

She jerked her attention back to Chloe. "Yeah?"

Chloe nodded toward the table of food. "Birthday girl gets to go first."

As she ate, laughed with her friends, took part in a hilarious game of pin the tail on the donkey and indulged in not one but two pieces of chocolate birthday cake, she had to guard against letting her gaze linger on Owen too long.

"You okay?"

She met Chloe's eyes across the table. "Yeah. Little overwhelmed by all this, I guess."

Chloe smiled. "Does it make you want to move to Blue Falls? As you can see, people are really nice here."

Linnea chuckled. "So you have ulterior motives?"

Chloe shrugged. "Perhaps."

There was something in that single word that gave Linnea pause, and she fought her first instinct to look in Owen's direction. Surely Chloe didn't know about what was going on between Linnea and Owen. They'd been careful about being discreet. Had there been something in the air the day Chloe almost caught them going at it in the kitchen? Or had Verona been spreading the news that they'd had pizza together at Gia's? The Linnea she'd been when she arrived told her this was yet another reason she should go home. When you had sex with someone in Dallas, the whole city didn't end up knowing it.

When Linnea tried to help clean up after the meal, Chloe smacked her hand away from the paper plates she was about to pick up.

"Nope. The birthday girl doesn't clean. She goes out on deck to enjoy the view."

Linnea started to argue, but Chloe threw up her hand to nix that idea. So instead of persisting, Linnea pulled her friend into a hug. "Thank you. This was great."

"That's what friends are for. Plus, I got cake."

With a smile, Linnea headed outside where most everyone else had migrated, as well. She made her way around to where the paddle wheel was churning the water at the back of the boat.

"Kind of neat, huh?"

The sound of Owen's voice made her smile before she turned to look at him leaning on the railing next to her. "Yeah. It's nice, old school."

"I'm surprised you like something that moves this slowly."

She shifted her attention back to the turning of the wheel. "I've learned it's nice to slow down sometimes, appreciate things instead of flying by them."

She realized she was talking about Owen more than anything else, and it struck her what that might mean. If she didn't hold herself in check, she was going to be in danger of falling for yet another man she couldn't have.

OWEN HUNG BACK as the rest of the party guests walked off the boat onto the dock. He realized he'd been staring at Linnea thanking everyone for coming to the party a moment before his sister came to stand beside him. He shifted his gaze, pretending that he'd been eyeing the two fake smokestacks atop the boat.

"So, when are you going to tell my best friend that you're falling for her?"

If he'd been eating or drinking anything, he would have no doubt choked. "What the hell was in that cake?"

"Don't play like you don't know what I'm talking about. I have two perfectly good eyes. You've been looking at Lin like you could have her for dessert."

He spun to look back across the lake. "We are not having this conversation."

"Doesn't change the fact that my baby brother has been bitten by the love bug."

"You're crazy."

"Am I?"

"Yes. I'm just being friendly. You said she needs friends right now."

"Friends, huh? I think you and I have different definitions. After all, you're the only one who got her a present."

"I didn't give her a present."

"Not yet. It's still sitting in the glove compartment of your truck."

He turned toward his sister and crossed his arms. "Are you snooping through my stuff? What the hell?"

"No. I saw you carry it out to the truck when you thought no one was looking. I don't know why you're being so sneaky about it."

"I wasn't being sneaky." Damn, if he'd known no one else was getting Linnea anything, he wouldn't have stopped in San Antonio on his way back from looking at a horse. He wouldn't have spent two hours searching for something that he thought she'd like.

Oh, hell, he was in danger of falling for her.

"You know me better than that," he said.

"I know you like people to think you can't feel something deep for someone else, but I'm your sister. I know better."

"Because I've shown I'm such a stick-with-one-woman kind of guy?"

She caught his gaze and held it. "No, because you try so hard not to stick with one woman. I think something inside you is yearning for more, but whether it's because of Katy or something else, you won't let yourself." She sighed. "It makes me sad."

Those words touched him deeper than he usually allowed any emotion to go. In fact, they stole his ability to respond for several seconds.

Chloe turned him to face her and gripped his upper arms. "Stop playing at being happy, and go for the real thing. I know it's scary, but it's worth it."

He thought about telling her she was crazy again, but he couldn't form the words. "I'm not sure I know how."

She smiled. "I promise you do."

He stared down at the only woman he'd allowed himself to love or trust in a long time. "You don't mind?"

"You and Lin? Why would I mind? I couldn't imagine a better person for her." She smiled. "Except maybe Garrett."

"Ouch."

Chloe laughed. "Just kidding. I want Garrett

to be happy, too, but he's not the one walking around like he's been hit with a stun gun."

He glanced beyond her to where Linnea was saying goodbye to Elissa and Cami. He couldn't have described any better how looking at Linnea made him feel.

Chloe lifted to her toes and kissed him on the cheek, then headed toward where Wyatt was waiting for her. The moment he saw his sister's hand slip into her husband's, a longing started beating inside Owen, a longing he feared only one woman was going to be able to satisfy.

WHEN LINNEA TURNED AWAY from thanking the boat owners for a lovely time, she noticed Chloe riding out of the parking lot with Wyatt. Just as she thought she was going to be hoofing it to the ranch, she noticed Owen leaning against the fender of his truck looking straight at her.

Her heart rate picked up speed as she negotiated the gangplank and walked toward him. "Looks like you're my ride back."

"Maybe if you ask nicely."

"Hey, I'm the birthday girl, remember?"

"Oh, yeah. I seem to recall something about that."

There was something different about him, but she couldn't put her finger on it.

"You want to go for a walk before we head back?"

Her blood danced through her body at the thought of being alone with him again. "Sure."

They hit the path that ran alongside the lake. When Owen took her hand in his, her heart pumped a little harder. It was such a simple thing for him to do, especially considering how much they'd already shared, but it seemed like an even bigger step somehow.

"Did you like your party?"

"Yeah. Everyone here is so incredibly nice."

They walked on, the dark deepening as they

moved farther away from the downtown lights. Owen stayed quiet, and Linnea didn't know if that was a good or bad thing. She did know that she really liked the feel of his hand engulfing hers.

"You okay?"

Owen glanced over at her before returning his attention to the path in front of them. "Just thinking about something Chloe said."

"Oh?"

He didn't answer immediately, instead guiding her to one of the benches that lined the path at intervals. Once they were sitting, he wrapped his arm around her shoulders and drew her close. "We haven't been as sneaky as we thought we were."

She jumped a little and leaned back to look up into his eyes. Though she couldn't see their color, she could envision the dark shades perfectly. That, in itself, should tell her it was time to get out of town. But she didn't want to, not one bit. "Chloe knows?"

"She at least suspects."

"What did she say?"

"That she was going to skin you alive for seducing her baby brother."

Linnea's mouth dropped open, which caused Owen to start laughing. "Why, you..." She punched him playfully in the stomach. "What did she really say?"

He grew more serious as he ran his thumb across the back of her hand. "She seems to think we should go for it."

"It?"

"Something more serious."

A shot of excitement raced through Linnea right before Owen looked out over the dark surface of the water.

"Even if that's what we both wanted, I don't know if I'm capable of more."

"Someone hurt you." It wasn't a question, because somehow she knew in the deepest part of her that it was the truth.

At first she thought he wasn't going to respond. It shouldn't have surprised her. After all, Owen Brody wasn't exactly a share-your-feelings sort of guy. He liked to act as though everything rolled off him with no ill effect, but no one was really like that.

"Listen, I'm not really into the whole psychoanalysis thing, but it's not really a secret that I don't do serious relationships." He took a deep breath. "I was serious about someone once, even thought I'd marry her, but it didn't work out."

"What happened?"

He glanced at her. "You really want to hear this?"

"You mean since my fiancé was already married and thus ruined my fairy-tale wedding plans? Sure, why not?" She was amazed at how much sarcasm she was able to put into her words without her heart feeling as if it were being carved into little pieces.

Owen smiled. "Too bad Michael didn't show up on the boat tonight. I think you might have tossed him overboard."

"That's not a bad idea."

Owen looked down at their entwined fingers and squeezed her hand. "I didn't think being a casual dater and nothing more was a conscious decision, but maybe it was." He leaned his head back and looked up at the sky before continuing. "I had a girlfriend in high school, Katy. She got pregnant, even though I had been smart enough to use protection. So I told her I'd marry her. So imagine my surprise when I climbed the tree next to her bedroom one night to find her in bed with Phillipe, the exchange student from France. Turned out I wasn't the father after all, and when I confronted her about it she said she'd a million times rather go to France with Phillipe and have an exciting life than be stuck in Blue Falls on a dirty ranch for the rest of her days."

Linnea didn't know this Katy person, but she sure wanted to smack her into next week. She could tell by the inflection of Owen's voice that he was repeating Katy's exact words, ones that still stuck with him all these years later.

"So she ended up in France?"

Owen snorted. "No. Phillipe went home early without telling her. She tried to make up with me, saying I was the father after all, but I wasn't dumb enough to fall for it. Last I heard she was married to a guy who works on an oil rig in the gulf and lives outside Kingsville."

Part of Linnea wanted to feel sorry for Katy for probably having to live a life that didn't give her much joy, of having her child's father run away to a foreign country, but she couldn't forgive how Katy had treated Owen when he'd been willing to take responsibility for the child, when he had obviously cared for her.

"She was a fool for not seeing what she had."

Owen looked at her as if he couldn't believe what he was hearing and didn't know what to say in response. Instead, he pulled her closer, cupped the back of her head and kissed her. She didn't need words, because that kiss said enough. He might never be a forever kind of guy, but he had a bigger heart than even he acknowledged.

She had no idea how long they kissed, but he eventually pulled back and dug something out of his pocket.

"I didn't realize people weren't getting you presents, but I got you something." He extended a small wrapped box.

"You didn't have to do that."

He shrugged. "What's a birthday without at least one present?"

She took the box and ripped off the wrapping paper. When she lifted the lid, her heart fluttered. Enough light shone from a nearby lamppost that she could see a necklace lying on a bed of cotton. It was shaped like a butterfly and had some sort of stone in the middle.

"It's a sapphire," Owen said as if it weren't any big deal.

But it was a big deal, enough that she brought her hand to her chest above her heart. "My birthstone."

"Yeah, I had to ask the lady at the store what it was. I had no idea."

Linnea looked up at Owen, who looked as if he felt a little awkward. "Thank you." Then she lifted her lips to his and kissed him so she wouldn't blurt out something more, like the fact that she was pretty sure she was beginning to fall in love with him.

Chapter Twelve

Owen kept waiting for Linnea to go home. Not that he wanted her to, but he'd gone and started feeling more for her than he should. And life had taught him that when you cared too much for someone, it hurt like hell itself when she was suddenly gone. He'd learned that at an early age, been burned by it again when he fell for Katy.

But no matter how much he tried to talk himself out of it, each day he felt himself wanting Linnea even more. And damn it, he found he wanted more than sneaking kisses and taking her in a barn. He halfway felt like cursing his sister for putting ideas into his head that he feared would lead to more heartache, for either him or Linnea. And they'd both had enough.

When he finished feeding the horses, he noticed Linnea standing at the entrance to the barn. The sight of the butterfly necklace resting against her skin caused an odd, expanding feeling inside him.

"You're up early," he said, trying to ignore the way she made him feel just looking at her.

She walked toward him, then slowly lifted her hand until Iris, their gentlest horse, could sniff her. "Does the offer to teach me to ride still stand?"

He watched as she visibly forced herself to stay close to the horse. "You sure?"

She hesitated a moment before nodding. "I feel like it's a good time to conquer my fear."

To start her off easy and make her feel safe, he saddled only one horse so they could ride together. When it came time for her to mount, however, he thought she might change her mind. But when she pressed her lips together and allowed him to help her into the saddle, pride welled up inside him. As they rode out of the barn and headed off toward the back of the ranch, he thought about how she'd faced the thing she feared most in order to move past it.

"Everything looks different from up here," she said as he guided their mount across the pasture.

"I can't even remember what it was like to look down from the top of a horse for the first time."

"Chloe told me once that your dad had you all up on horses while you were still in diapers."

"Yep. It's as natural to me as walking."

Linnea reached forward and ran her hand down the side of the horse's neck. "Who knows? Maybe I'll get really good at this."

Something warm bloomed to life inside him

and radiated out from his middle. He liked the idea of her riding this ranch with him.

She looked over her shoulder. "You okay?"

"Yeah, why?"

"Because you just sucked in your breath."

He had? "It's nothing."

But he knew that was a lie, even if he didn't remember doing it. As they continued to ride, him showing her the ranch that was as much a part of him as the blood in his veins, he enjoyed the feel of his arms and legs around her. When she asked questions about the ranch and everything he, Garrett and their dad did on their acreage, she sounded genuinely interested. She wasn't just being a city girl pretending to care what the country folk did. For the first time since her arrival, she actually looked as though she belonged here.

But this being her first ride, he could tell when she needed a break. He reined in the horse and dismounted, then helped her down to the ground, holding her close after she slid down his body. Before he let her go, he dropped his lips to hers and kissed her as if he'd never see her again.

When he pulled away, she smiled up at him. "That's some kiss. I should try something new every day if that's my reward."

He tied the horse's reins around a branch of the largest live oak tree on the ranch, then stepped up behind Linnea as she stared out across acres of his family's land.

"It's stark but pretty at the same time," she said.

The warmth in his chest grew, and he kissed the top of her head. He wondered if this was how his dad had felt when he held his mom. That thought sent such a shock through him that he stepped away from Linnea, needing to break contact so he could shove aside the feelings he was having toward her. Ones that could leave him as devastated as his dad had been when he lost the love of his life.

An old guilt twisted Owen's gut as he took several steps away from Linnea, giving life to an irrational fear that he was a danger to this woman who was coming to mean too much to him.

He jumped when Linnea touched his upper arm.

"What's wrong?"

He shook his head. "Nothing."

"I don't believe you."

He managed to stop a sharp reply before it escaped. She didn't deserve that when she hadn't done anything wrong. As he looked down into her kind eyes, he suddenly wanted to confess everything, to finally expose the wound that had been festering for almost as long as he could remember.

"It's stupid."

"Not if it's bothering you like it obviously is."

He shifted his gaze away, staring out toward part of his family's cattle herd in the distance. Linnea slipped her hands into his.

"You've already seen me at my worst," she said.

He took a deep breath. "I've never admitted this to anyone, but getting close to people scares me."

"Because of Katy."

He shook his head, wondering if he could really give his deepest, darkest secret a voice. "My mom."

Linnea's forehead creased. "I don't understand. She was killed by a hit-and-run driver."

The pain he'd felt when his dad had told him the news felt as raw as it had that night, and he swallowed hard. "But do you know why she was out that night?"

Linnea shook her head.

"I was sick, coughing a lot, and Mom went to

town to get some cough syrup for me. She was on her way back when she was hit."

Linnea's hands tightened on his. "Oh, Owen. I'm so sorry, but it wasn't your fault."

"My brain knows that."

"But your heart feels differently."

He nodded once. "When things fell apart with Katy, it felt like I was being punished again for caring for someone. Consciously or unconsciously, it's why I've never gotten close to anyone else. I know that sounds crazy."

"Our minds play cruel tricks on us," she said. "When Danielle came into my store and told me about Michael, I thought it was a horrible lie. And when I realized it wasn't, I felt as if I must be the most stupid person in the world for not seeing the truth."

He lifted his hand from her grasp and caressed her cheek. "You are anything but stupid."

"I know that now. I mean, there are times

when I still question how I couldn't have seen it, but others when I realize that bad things just happen through no fault of our own. It sucks, but that's life."

She hadn't said anything he didn't know already, but something about hearing someone else say it, someone who wasn't invested in his feelings of guilt, lifted a weight inside him. Unable to articulate everything that was coming to the surface inside him, he instead pulled Linnea close and kissed her deeply, their lips and tongues not able to get enough of each other.

But despite how great she felt in his arms, he couldn't dispel the feeling of dread that had formed a knot in his stomach.

LINNEA DIDN'T THINK she'd ever felt better in her life as she and Owen stared out across the simple beauty of the ranch. He sat with his back against the live oak tree while she was snuggled between his legs with his arms wrapped around her.

"This is so peaceful," she said.

"You really don't miss the hustle and bustle of Dallas?"

She thought about it for a moment. "Honestly, no. I've never thought of myself as a country girl, but being here has been just what I needed."

But she'd already been at the Brodys' ranch much longer than she'd planned and couldn't put off returning to her responsibilities much longer. Or could she? She thought again of the space available in downtown Blue Falls, but she didn't mention it to Owen. Though he'd shared a lot with her, she still didn't know if they could have any sort of future together. While the thought of not having him close caused her heart to hurt, she had to take a mental step back and think about what she needed, separate from any possible romantic relationships.

She needed to make decisions that would make her happy, give her a future that would bring her joy in her work.

"I hate to spoil the moment, but I need to get back to the barn," Owen said. "I've got a potential buyer for one of the horses coming by later."

She turned in his arms to look up at him. "Really? That's awesome."

He smiled as though her words were worth more than all the money in Texas.

Before he helped her mount the horse again, he pulled her close and kissed her.

"That never gets old," she said when he ended the kiss.

"No, it doesn't."

Linnea couldn't stop smiling as they rode back to the main part of the ranch, then took care of the horses. As they started to leave the barn, Owen grabbed her and pushed her up against the inside wall. His lips came down to claim hers. No matter how many times he kissed her, it never failed to send a thrill racing along her veins.

The sound of an approaching vehicle found its way past thoughts of making love to Owen again, causing her to break the kiss and push gently against his chest. Only then did he seem to hear it, too. When he glanced around the edge of the doorway, he frowned in confusion.

"What is it?" If it was Michael again, she was going to walk out of this barn with a pitchfork to get her point across.

"It's Simon." Owen stepped away from her and headed out to greet the sheriff.

As she followed Owen, Simon looked between the both of them. She wondered if what Owen had said after her party was true, that perhaps they weren't hiding their relationship nearly as well as they thought they were.

"Hey, Simon," Owen said. "What brings you out here?"

Simon shifted from one booted foot to the other, looking distinctly uncomfortable. Oh, God, had something happened to one of the Brodys?

"There are some days when I hate my job," Simon said, almost as if an internal thought had unwittingly tumbled from his mouth. "Michael Benson filed assault charges against you, and since you punched him with dozens of witnesses I don't have any choice."

"About what?" Owen asked.

Dread settled in Linnea's middle.

"I'm here to arrest you."

Owen snorted a laugh, but when Simon didn't join in, Owen stopped abruptly. "You're serious."

"I'm afraid so."

"That bastard."

"We'll get things sorted out, but I have to go through the motions for now."

"What, you going to handcuff me?"

"You planning on making a run for it?"

Linnea stepped in between the two men and held up a hand. "Wait. How can he do this? He's the one who was harassing me."

Simon looked at her with sympathy and understanding, and she realized she was looking at a man who was trapped by sworn duty.

"Because he didn't hit you or threaten you. And there's no restraining order against him."

This time, she cursed. Even after everything Michael had done, she'd never imagined he'd stoop this low to get back at her. How could he not see he was the one at fault?

Linnea turned toward Owen. "Don't worry. I'll fix this."

Owen reached out and cupped her face, seeming not to care that Simon saw the affectionate gesture. "I don't want you going anywhere near Michael."

She was saved from having to make that

promise by his dad and Garrett returning from town with a load of feed.

"This is nonsense," his dad said after Owen explained what was going on.

The look on Wayne's face broke Linnea's heart. "I'm so sorry about this."

"That is also nonsense," he said as he wrapped a strong arm around her shoulders as they watched Simon escort Owen to the patrol car.

She wanted to scream as the door closed and he looked out at her with a smile she knew was meant to make her feel better. But she wasn't going to feel better until she made this right, until she ensured that Michael Benson was out of her life and the lives of everyone she cared about for good.

When Garrett said he was going into the house to contact an attorney and then to the bank to arrange for bail, she grabbed his arm to stop him. "No, I'll do that because none of this would have happened if I hadn't come here and imposed on your hospitality." She glanced toward the barn, then back at Garrett. "But there is something you can do. A potential buyer is coming by later to look at Galahad. Make sure that sale goes through. Talk that horse up like your life depends on it."

"Shouldn't we just reschedule?"

"No. This is important to Owen, and I believe it's the beginning of a successful business for him."

"You think he's going to stick with it?"

"Your brother isn't as uncommitted as you think. It just took him longer to find what he wanted out of life."

"So it seems." Owen's dad looked at her as though he knew how close she and Owen had become.

Her heart rate accelerated as she considered that maybe Owen was falling as much as she was. She'd told him from the beginning that she didn't expect commitment from him, but then she'd only thought they'd spend the one night together. With each moment since then that they'd spent anywhere near each other, she'd fallen for him even more.

By the time she met with an attorney to represent Owen, her head was filled with plans to rid themselves of Michael once and for all. Unfortunately, it meant that she had to leave Owen in jail a little longer than she planned, because if he got even a hint of what she intended to do, he'd try to stop her. And while she might not really be the cause of the current situation, it wouldn't have come to his door if she hadn't. If she wanted to see if she and Owen had a real chance, she had to do this.

By the time she outlined all of her plans to Chloe, her friend looked stunned. "You thought of all this since Simon came to get Owen?"

"I guess I work well under pressure."

"And you're sure about all this?"

"Positive."

When Linnea stood and headed for the door, Chloe came around her desk and pulled her into her arms.

"Be careful, okay? Don't take any unnecessary chances."

"Don't worry. I'm not underestimating Michael anymore."

She headed to the ranch, hoping that Garrett and his dad didn't question her about why she was leaving. When she arrived, Mr. Brody was in the kitchen cooking steaks and potatoes. He looked up at her entrance, but his eyes dimmed when he looked beyond her.

"They didn't let Owen out?"

"That's next on the list. I just came by to get my things first."

He turned toward her. "You're leaving?"

"Yes, I have to take care of some things in Dallas."

"Oh?"

"Yes. I've left Katrina with the full load at work for too long."

He looked as though he wanted to say more, and she would swear she could see him change what he was going to say midstream. "Are you coming back?"

"I won't be a stranger." Part of her wanted to tell him her plans, but she had to keep it quiet until she knew for sure they would work out the way she hoped.

He walked around the table and pulled her into his arms much as his daughter had done. She blinked against tears as she realized that Owen wasn't the only Brody she'd come to care for even more since her arrival.

"You've got a place here anytime, you hear?"

"Thank you."

As she hurried from the house, she met Garrett coming up the front steps. Beyond him, she saw a truck with a horse trailer leaving. She smiled as she saw Galahad's dark tail swish in the back.

"They took the horse?"

Garrett held up several hundred-dollar bills. "Owen's first sale. I guess he's officially in business."

She met Garrett's eyes, which were a lot like his younger brother's. "Thank you."

"I think I should be the one thanking you."

"Why?"

"Because you made me see beyond the surface with my brother. I'll do whatever I can to make sure he's a success at this."

Her heart expanded as she lifted to her toes and kissed him on the cheek.

When she stepped back, he held her gaze. "You love him, don't you?"

There was no use denying it when it was probably written all over her face. "Yes, I do. But I haven't told him that yet."

He glanced down at her bag. "Do you intend to?"

"I hope to, if he feels the same way."

"He does."

Her heart leaped. "Did he say that?"

"No. But I've got eyes, and I've never seen my brother act this way about a woman."

"Act how?"

He smiled. "Like he's annoyed that he has to waste hours sleeping."

Garrett's words repeated in her head as she drove to the sheriff's department. When she got there, she sat in the parking lot for a few minutes, making a couple of calls and trying to get her burgeoning excitement under control. A lot of puzzle pieces still had to fit perfectly for her plan to work, but she couldn't prevent the hope swelling inside her.

When she finally walked inside, she asked to speak to Simon privately. He escorted her into his office and closed the door. She handed over the necessary money to post Owen's bail. Then she extended a sealed envelope.

"What's this?"

"Something that I hope you'll be able to shred without reading if the next couple of days go as planned. So don't open it unless you hear from Chloe to do so."

"Okay, that sounds mysterious. I'm not sure I like it."

"Don't worry. Just some insurance on my part."

Simon stared at her for several seconds, but she didn't cave and tell him what was in the envelope.

"I'll go let Owen out," he said.

"Could you wait a few minutes, please?"

Simon settled back in his seat. "Linnea, you're not going to do something stupid like go back to Michael, are you?"

"Heavens no."

"Good." Then he gave her a shrewd look.

"But you do have something up your sleeve, and I wouldn't like it if you told me what it was, would I?"

"I can't begin to imagine being able to read your mind, Sheriff."

"Uh-huh." He shook his head. "Just don't do anything to put yourself in danger. And if you need my help in any way, don't hesitate to call me."

"If you can give me thirty minutes before you release Owen, that will be enough. Thank you."

He still didn't look as if he liked her unspoken plan, but he couldn't stop her.

She forced herself not to look toward the doorway that led back to the holding cells as she left the sheriff's office. As she drove out of Blue Falls, the hope that had been vibrating inside her acquired a roommate named Anxiety. She did her best to bolster the former and dispel the latter as she pointed her car toward Dallas.

Chapter Thirteen

Owen paced the cell, unable to sit still. As much as he'd rabble-roused throughout the years, he'd managed to never end up behind bars. Then he tried to protect a woman from unwanted advances, and that's what landed him in jail. And being locked up wasn't the worst part. It was thinking about not being out where he could protect the woman he loved.

He stopped pacing as the weight of that realization hit him square in the chest. During all their time together, he'd told himself it was just two consenting adults having fun. But it was more than that, and probably had been since they spent their first night together.

He ran his hand over his face. Despite his determination to do otherwise, he'd allowed her into his heart. He cursed when he thought about what that meant. Despite her time away from it, her life was in Dallas. She had a business, a home, family. And he was on the cusp of really making a go of his business.

"Damn it."

He'd had an appointment this afternoon with a potential buyer for Galahad. If he was a no-show, word would get around that he was as undependable as most people thought. Most people, but not Linnea. She'd believed in his vision from the moment he told her about it. Maybe that had actually been when he started falling head over heels for her.

He walked to the front of the cell and leaned his forehead against the cold bars, resisting the urge to bang his head for being such an idiot.

He and Linnea got along great. Goodness knew the sex was out of this world. But even if his business did start to build, he couldn't give her the life she was used to. She was a city girl used to nice things.

Only she hadn't seemed to mind spending time at the ranch, time with him. What would she say if he told her he loved her? He thought maybe she felt the same, but he couldn't be sure without laying his cards on the table. Did he really want to take that risk? He sighed, trying to decide if he was ready to open himself up to potential pain again.

Yes. The word bubbled up from somewhere deep in his mind, echoing louder and louder until it nearly drowned out the sound of Simon walking into the room with a ring of keys.

"You've been sprung, my friend."

Owen's heartbeat thudded a little harder as he thought that Linnea probably stood on the other side of the doorway Simon had just walked through. No matter what happened, he knew he had to tell her the truth about how he felt. Damn, he'd been less afraid to climb onto cantankerous horses and even a couple of bulls during his brief stint on the rodeo circuit. But there were much better rewards to be had if she felt the same way.

But when he walked out into the main room of the sheriff's office, it wasn't Linnea waiting for him but rather his sister. "Where's Linnea?"

"She had to take care of some business stuff."

He was surprised by how hard that revelation hit him. She was talking fancy wedding dresses and bottom lines while he sat in jail for slugging her ex? He mentally shook himself, knowing that he wasn't being fair. After all, she'd been there for him as he worked toward building his business, even given him a lot of good ideas. And he knew how much she loved her store.

But when Chloe dropped him off at the ranch

and he found out that Linnea had left without saying anything to him, he felt as if he'd been punched in the gut. And then fear swamped him.

"She's gone to confront Michael." He spun to retrace his steps. The guy was crazy. What had she been thinking going up there alone?

"She'll come back," his father said, stopping Owen in his tracks.

"Did she say that?"

When he saw the look in his father's eyes, Owen realized what his storming toward the door had said without him speaking a word. Though he'd tried to tell himself it wasn't possible, he'd fallen in love with Linnea. The question was, did she feel the same way? She'd said she only wanted a fling, but he'd had no-strings sex before. What they'd shared lately was a lot more than that.

"Not in so many words."

Owen didn't move as that sank in. It didn't

matter. Even if their time together was over, there was no way he was letting her put herself in danger because of him.

LINNEA TOOK SEVERAL SLOW, deep breaths before she entered the downtown building that held the offices of Michael's financial services firm. Her heels clicked on the marble lobby floor as she crossed from the security desk to the elevator. She'd dressed in one of her favorite outfits, making sure she looked the way Michael was used to seeing her so, hopefully, this time the message got across. Of course, the carefully crafted plans she'd mapped out in record time were really her ace in the hole. The edge of her mouth twitched as a well of empowerment rose inside her. She was putting Michael in his place, and he'd damn well better stay there.

When she stepped off the elevator into the lobby of Wiseman Financial Group on the seventeenth floor, she took another breath and walked past the empty receptionist desk, straight into Michael's office. He was on the phone, but his eyes widened when he saw her and he quickly ended the call.

He smiled as he leaned back in his leather chair. "I knew you'd come back."

Anger burst to life like an inferno inside her, but she didn't let it show. "So confident that you had to have Owen arrested." She made a dismissive sound.

Michael's smile faded. "You needed to see him for what he really is, a violent man."

"I've learned a lot about seeing people for who they really are lately, and Owen Brody is a million times better man than you'll ever be. You will be dropping those charges against him."

"I won't."

"That's what I expected you to say." She reached into her handbag and pulled out an envelope and held it up. "You will drop the charges, and you will stay away from me, my family, the Brodys, all of my friends and my business. You will not contact or harass any of us in any way. It will be like you don't exist. If not, I'll march down the hall and give this to Mr. Wiseman. It details how you tried to marry me even though you are already married, how you've harassed me on more than one occasion since I found out about your duplicity and that you trespassed on land owned by the Brody family."

He started to speak, but she held up her hand.

"There are identical letters already addressed and ready to be sent to every member of your board of directors and every major media outlet in Dallas and San Francisco." She smiled. "Yes, I know where your other life is."

"You're bluffing. You aren't this type of person."

"What, the type to stand up for myself? That's where you're wrong."

Michael's expression darkened. "You even breathe a word of that to anyone, and you'll regret it."

Linnea smiled slowly. "I was hoping you'd say something like that." She tapped the lapel of her jacket. "I'm recording this conversation. Oh, and I left another letter with the sheriff in Blue Falls. Should anything even remotely suspicious happen to me, my friends or my family, I've named you as suspect number one. And if I'm not back downstairs within ten minutes, Katrina has instructions to call the police and tell them I'm being held against my will. How would that look when the police storm the office and haul you away?"

Michael looked as if he were staring at someone he didn't recognize. At least he knew what it felt like now. "You're serious?"

"As the proverbial heart attack." She waved

the envelope. "Now, do we have an understanding?"

Michael sat and stared at her with hatred burning in his eyes, but he finally nodded.

"Say it so I have it for the recording."

His eyes narrowed as he said, "We have an understanding. I won't bother you, your family or friends again."

"Good." She slipped the envelope back into her bag. "I, in turn, will not contact you in any way. I have, however, provided Danielle with a full, written account of events that was requested by her attorney."

"You did what?" Michael's anger bubbled over.

She caught his gaze and held it. "I told the truth, Michael, which is more than I can say for you. Be glad I've given you the option of keeping your fancy position here. But don't doubt for an instant that if you slip even a fraction of your toe across the agreement lines we've drawn here today, I'll do everything in my power to make sure you lose that, as well."

With that, she headed toward the door with a sense of satisfaction that was off the charts.

"I'm glad I didn't get stuck with you," Michael said, sounding petty and childish.

When she looked back at him, she smiled just to irritate him further. "I assure you, the feeling is mutual."

She strode through the lobby and into the elevator. As soon as the doors closed, it was all she could do not to perform a little victory dance.

When she slipped into Katrina's car a couple of minutes later, her friend looked relieved.

"How did it go?"

"I don't think I'm going to have to worry about Michael anymore."

"Are you sure?"

"He might have fooled me about a lot of things, but I have absolute confidence that the one thing he won't risk is his posh position."

And it struck her how incredibly sad that was, that Michael was so used to getting what he wanted through lies and smooth talking that he'd actually thought he could convince her to return to him even after she knew the truth. But even more important than her was the lifestyle he was accustomed to living. She was ashamed she'd gotten so caught up in it, as well, but spending time at the Brody ranch had reminded her of what was really important.

"Well, I'd say this calls for a celebratory lunch," Katrina said.

Linnea shoved away thoughts of Michael, telling herself that as soon as his building faded in the rearview mirror, she was well and truly done with him. "That sounds like an excellent idea."

After they'd ordered their meals and a bottle of champagne at La Fontaine, Linnea took a deep breath, one that felt so free she couldn't help but smile. Now for the next phase of her plan, the part that had changed as she drove to Dallas. "I'd like to talk to you about something."

"Okay, that's your serious tone."

Linnea smiled. "Nothing bad. Actually, it could be something quite wonderful if everything goes as planned."

Katrina leaned forward. "I'm sufficiently intrigued."

"How would you feel about buying out my portion of the shop?"

"What?" Katrina couldn't have looked more shocked if Linnea had told her she was going to live among gorillas in Africa like Dian Fossey.

"Staying in Blue Falls has made me realize that I'm ready for a big change, and there's a storefront there that I'm hoping to acquire and start a new shop. I've already got so many ideas that my brain can barely contain them all."

"You're serious?"

"I am, but if you don't want to do this, we'll work something else out."

"But you're moving to Blue Falls?"

Linnea paused for a moment, wondering if she could be making another mistake with such a leap so soon after being hurt by Michael. But she'd thought about it all the way to Dallas, and she'd realized that even if she and Owen didn't have a future together, she needed this change of venue. And the more she thought about starting a new store, the more excited she became. If it didn't work out with Owen, it would hurt but she'd survive. She'd already been through one fire and lived to tell the tale, had come out the other side even stronger than before.

Finally, she nodded. "Yeah, I am. I really like it there. It's small but has a nice tourist trade. The people are wonderful, and a bridal shop would fit in perfectly with the eclectic mix of downtown businesses."

"Does this have anything to do with Owen?"

The question startled Linnea. "Why would you say that?"

"Because when you've called the past couple of times, you talked about him more than Chloe."

Linnea leaned against the back of her chair. "Only partially."

"You've fallen for someone else?" Katrina sounded worried, and Linnea couldn't blame her.

"I think so, but I would want to make this move even if I knew we wouldn't share one more minute together. I can't fully explain it, but the moment I walked into that empty store space, I felt as if it was meant to be mine. I know that sounds crazy, but it's the truth."

"It's not crazy to go after what you want. I just worry about you getting involved with someone so soon after the worm who shall not be named."

Linnea smiled at her friend's description of

Michael. "I know. Don't think I haven't thought about it a lot, but Owen Brody is as honest as they come. He's hardworking in a real, hands-on sort of way. He's funny, down to earth. Protective, but not overbearing."

"So basically the polar opposite of you know who."

"Yeah." Linnea grinned at the flood of memories of her time with Owen. "Not to mention he's very good in bed."

Katrina gave a short burst of laughter that was so loud it drew the glances of other diners before she covered her mouth. After a few seconds, she leaned forward. "Well, I can't recall ever hearing you say that."

Michael hadn't been a bad lover, but Owen had woken something inside her, a sort of primal wildness that she hadn't known existed. There were times she was with him when it was really difficult to keep her hands to herself.

And the fact that he seemed to feel the same way only fueled her desire.

"And your face is getting red." Katrina laughed a little. "I hope it works out for you."

"So, you're interested in becoming sole owner of the shop?"

"If that's what you want, then yeah."

They talked about the specifics of the sale and transition while they waited for their food. By the time the waiter placed her halibut and risotto in front of her, she realized she was starving. Since leaving Blue Falls, she'd had nothing more than a bag of peanuts from a gas station. She'd been, by turns, too nervous or too angry to eat anything. But now that the anxiety about confronting Michael and broaching the subject of selling her business to Katrina was behind her, she felt she could put away as much food as a football team.

Before they returned to the shop, they made stops at the attorney's office and the bank to get the ball rolling on the transition. The sooner they could sign on the dotted line, the sooner she could start working on her new dream in Blue Falls.

When they finally did return to the shop, it felt as if she'd been away forever. While what she'd built could still bring a smile to her face, the comfortable rightness of it wasn't quite the same as it had been before. Whether this was because she was here when she'd found out about Michael's marriage or the fact that her heart was already somewhere else, she wasn't sure. Maybe it was a little of both.

OWEN WALKED OUT of the barn after working with the new horse he'd bought with his proceeds from selling Galahad. He was thankful that Garrett had taken care of that sale for him, that he and his dad seemed to have had a change of heart where his horse-training business was concerned. He suspected that had a lot to do with Linnea, and he was thankful for her support, as well. That he had the support of his family should have made him happy, but it felt as if happiness had left town riding shotgun in Linnea's car. He could kick himself for getting so involved with her when he'd known she'd eventually leave.

He looked up just before he barreled into Chloe.

"Hello, baby brother," she said.

"Hey, Chloe." He skirted her and kept heading toward the house.

"Glad you're so happy to see me."

He realized he was being an ass, and Linnea's leaving wasn't Chloe's fault. "Sorry. What's up?"

She crossed her arms. "What's got you in such a nasty mood?"

"Lot on my mind."

"That include Linnea?"

"I didn't say that."

"Come on, it doesn't take a genius to figure out that your pissy mood started when she left."

"Maybe I'm just ticked off because I got thrown in jail. Can't say that was on my bucket list."

"That wasn't her fault."

"I know that." He sighed when he realized how much he'd raised his voice at Chloe. None of the feelings twisting inside him were her fault, either.

"You love her, don't you?"

"It doesn't matter."

"It does matter."

He stared right into her eyes. "It doesn't. I went to Dallas to make sure she was safe, and she was. The end."

Chloe's forehead creased. "Did she say something to upset you?"

"I didn't talk to her."

"You drove all the way to Dallas and didn't even talk to her?"

He shifted his gaze to the Penningtons' ranch across the road. "When I finally found her, she was at the shop. Laughing. I figured she must have gotten back to her familiar surroundings and realized how happy they made her."

"So you left?"

"Yeah. It was just a fling between two consenting adults, no big deal."

"That's not true, and you know it." Chloe took a few steps toward him. "You love her, and she loves you. It's as obvious as that herd of cattle on the hill."

"You're smart, Chloe, but you're wrong about this."

"She's not Katy Mulligan."

He jerked his gaze to his sister's. "I know that."

"I know Katy did a number on you, and that's why you've been Mr. Play the Field ever since."

"That was a long time ago."

"And I know losing Mom is part of the equation, too. You're not the only one it messed with. I thought about how much it hurt to lose her when I started falling for Wyatt. It was part of the reason I fought it so hard." She glanced toward the house. "Garrett's the same, though he hides it a different way."

"I should have stuck to how I've always done things. I'm the wild child of the family, right? The one who can't settle on anyone or anything."

"That's not you anymore. You've got a business off the ground and running, and you finally gave your heart to someone again."

He started to object, but she held up her hand to stop him.

"Don't judge Linnea before you know all the facts."

He looked at her and saw something just below the surface. "You know something."

She held up both of her hands, palms out. "That's all I'm saying."

"Come on, out with it."

Before she could respond again, his phone rang. With a growl, he fished it off his belt and answered without even looking at the display.

"Hey, good news," Simon Teague said in Owen's ear. "Linnea's asshat ex dropped the charges against you."

It took a moment for the words to sink in. "Really?"

"Yep. You're free and clear."

After Owen ended the call, he stared at the phone for a moment.

"What's wrong?"

Chloe's question reminded him she was still standing there. "Michael dropped the assault charges against me."

When Chloe didn't say anything, he raised his eyes to find her smiling. "Linnea?"

She just kept smiling as she walked past him, playfully swatting him on the chest. "Told you so."

Owen continued standing in the same spot as Chloe got in her car and headed home. Gradually, a smile took over his lips. Maybe he did have a chance with Linnea after all.

Chapter Fourteen

Linnea took a slow, deep breath to calm her nerves, then applied the pen to the paper that would make her the newest occupant of Blue Falls' Main Street. She felt every bit as anxious and excited as she had when she signed for the loan to open the shop in Dallas. Telling herself this was the right thing to do, she signed her name on the stack of forms.

Justine took the paperwork and handed over the keys. "Congratulations."

"Thanks." She looked up into the smiling faces of Chloe, India and Keri, who'd all gathered around the small table next to the front window of the Mehlerhaus Bakery.

"I feel like I should have some confetti to throw," Keri said.

"No need. But I will take one of those big devil's food cupcakes."

"Coming right up."

After Justine left with the signed forms, Linnea's friends pulled up chairs to the table, all with their own sweet treats to celebrate.

"So, how does it feel?" Chloe asked.

"Great and scary all rolled into one."

"Well, I for one am glad it's done. You have no idea how hard it's been to avoid my brother's questions while you were gone."

"Sorry. I just wanted to make sure everything worked out before I said anything."

"So, what are you going to say now that you are officially a resident?"

"I don't know. I guess I'll find out when I call him."

"Just wing it," Keri said. "The right thing will come out."

Linnea laughed. "I'm not so sure about that. I've run through dozens of scenarios, and I still don't know what to say."

"No time like the present to try one out," Chloe said, a mischievous grin tugging at her lips.

After her friends returned to work, Linnea kept thinking about what she was going to say to Owen and how, especially when he hadn't said anything about being in love with her, either. Maybe she could just ease into it, start with something that didn't have anything to do with the two of them. Chloe was right, though. No time like the present. She picked up her phone and dialed Owen's number.

Half an hour later, her heart leaped as she saw Owen walk in the front door of the bakery. She smiled wide but kept her seat, unsure how he would react if she hopped up and hugged him the way she wanted to.

"Hey," she said, feeling awkward and nervous.

"Hi."

Her smile faltered a little at his simple response. "It's good to see you."

"You, too. Was surprised to get your call." He shifted on his feet, as if he wasn't sure he was staying, before slipping onto the chair across from her.

Linnea slid a wrapper with two spice cookies in it toward him. "Got your favorite cookies for you."

He looked up at her with a questioning expression.

"I'm sorry I didn't call while I was gone."

"It's okay." He acted as if it was no big deal, and for a moment she wondered if she'd just made a series of horrible mistakes. Could she live in a town the size of Blue Falls and not be with the man she loved?

But there was something about how he was holding himself, on the edge of the chair as if he might bolt for the door at any moment, that gave her hope. Was he shielding himself because he thought what they had was over and he didn't want it to be? While her mind was sifting through all the possibilities, he looked up and caught her gaze.

"Did you have anything to do with Michael dropping the charges against me?"

She nodded. "You won't have to worry about him anymore. Neither will I."

He looked at her a little more intently. "Should I ask?"

She laughed a little. "I didn't do anything I could be arrested for, don't worry."

"Good."

"But it's amazing what can happen if you apply pressure in just the right place." She told him about the ultimatum she'd given Michael and how she'd planned it so carefully that she, his family and hers were all safe from Michael.

"You think he'll stick to the promise?"

"Trust me. The last thing he wants is to lose the nice income he has. I think he's going to need it, considering what Danielle has planned for him."

Owen laughed, and the knot that had been sitting in the middle of Linnea's chest relaxed.

"You have time to go for a short walk?" she asked.

"Sure."

As they headed for the door, Linnea looked beyond the display case full of treats to where Keri was giving her two thumbs-ups and a giant smile. Linnea had to press her lips together to keep from laughing.

When they were out on the sidewalk, Linnea started walking toward the store she now owned two doors down. "I didn't just go to Dallas to deal with Michael."

"I know you had to get back to your business."

"Yes, I did, but not for the reason you think." She stopped in front of the empty store and turned to face the big display window. "I went to make arrangements to sell my part of the business to my partner so I could buy this. I'm going to start a new bridal store here, and I'll be working with Keri, Skyler and Elissa on coordinating different wedding services."

Owen took a step toward the store, then turned back to look at her. "You're moving to Blue Falls?"

She shoved away the concern that she had perhaps just freaked him out and held up her key to the front door. "Would you like to see?"

"I've been inside before."

"Oh, okay."

"But not when it's empty."

Her hope that had taken a dip a moment before surged again as she hurried to the door and opened it. Owen's boots echoed against the wooden floor, and she found herself hoping that she'd get to hear that sound a lot in the future. She wasn't going to push him, especially after she'd assured him that she didn't expect commitment. But that didn't mean her heart didn't hope for their relationship to eventually grow into more. She was already in love with Owen. She just had to wait to see if he eventually felt the same. And if he didn't, she still had to believe that this move was the right thing to do. It felt right.

She led him through the building, sharing her plans for her new store. She'd been the owner of the building less than an hour, and she could hardly wait to start ordering display cases, shelving and, best of all, the beautiful products she would sell to brides-to-be. She took a moment to envision the end result and was so glad that her experience with Michael hadn't ruined her love of weddings forever.

When she finally got to the back of the building and realized she'd been talking nonstop, she turned to face Owen, who looked a little shell-shocked by the barrage of details she'd thrown at him. "Sorry. I guess I'm a little excited."

"It's okay. You deserve this."

But even as he said he was happy for her, her excitement dimmed a little. In her imaginings, when she'd told him about staying in Blue Falls, he'd swept her into his arms and confessed his love for her. But she realized that was a silly romantic fantasy, a fairy tale. She had to be okay with real life, no matter how much part of her still yearned for the fairy tale. But she'd already planned one fairy-tale happily ever after only to discover it had been built on lies. She'd take real life built on truth any day.

Owen walked slowly toward the far corner and then turned back toward her. "You should contact Ryan Teague, Simon's brother. He does beautiful woodwork. I bet he could make you some pretty cabinets and counter space that would have more personality than something you could buy through a catalog."

It might not be a declaration of love, but Owen's suggestion showed that he did care about her at some level. She could tell herself all day that she was okay with living her new life alone, but her heart was begging her to make an effort toward what she really wanted—a life with Owen.

THE NEXT TWO weeks went by in a blur. From early in the morning until late at night, Linnea was busy settling into her new life. She considered it a good sign that she'd made the right decision when her condo sold within two days of her listing it. So she made a quick trip to Dallas for the closing and to arrange for movers to pack up her things and deliver them to her new apartment above the Blue Falls store.

While in Dallas, she had gone to her parents' house for dinner to find her entire family there. She could tell they were concerned about the abrupt changes in her life the moment she stepped through the front door.

Her mom was the first to say something when Linnea accompanied her into the kitchen to carry food into the dining room. "Don't you think you're rushing into this, honey? I mean, you just went through an awful experience. This feels so drastic."

Linnea placed her hand on her mother's forearm and looked beyond to where her father had entered the room. "Trust me when I say I've thought about this a lot. This is something I really want. I can't wait to have the store up and running so you all can come see it."

As she now looked at her boxes piled high on the sides of her new apartment, she knew it was going to be at least a month before she should have everything fixed just how she wanted it before her family descended to make sure she was doing okay.

The sound of banging and male voices on the first floor drew her from her thoughts, and she hurried down the stairs. The sight that greeted her reminded her of something she'd seen on TV about an Amish community coming together to build a barn. It felt as though every guy she knew in Blue Falls was busy installing her cabinetry that Ryan and his brothers had arrived with that morning.

"I still can't believe you got all this built so quickly," she said as she approached Ryan and his brother Nathan.

"Amazing what you can do when you have a taskmaster for a sister-in-law." He grinned as he looked over his shoulder to where Keri was placing a box of muffins and donuts on one of the newly installed display cases.

"I heard that, Ryan Teague," Keri said.

Linnea's heart filled with love for all the people surrounding her, helping literally build her new life. A different type of love swelled her heart when she made eye contact with Owen, who stood a few feet away taking a drink of water. The intensity in his gaze made her wonder if he was thinking about the times they'd made love, if perhaps he was planning a repeat performance. They hadn't been together that way since she told him about moving to Blue Falls. For a few days after that, she'd wondered if maybe their time together was in the past. But then he'd arrived with a bouquet of bright orange lilies and finally kissed her again. She'd wanted to sing and dance, but she still wasn't willing to lay all her cards on the table.

She counted it a good sign, however, when Chloe gave her a knowing smile late in the afternoon before vacating the premises, leaving only Owen. He looked as though he was about to leave, as well. Wanting to take another tentative step toward being able to tell him the truth about how she felt, she approached him.

"Thanks for all your help," she said.

"No problem."

"I know you have a lot of work of your own and you don't have to be here."

Owen closed the distance between them and pulled her into his arms. It felt so good to be so close to him again.

"How about you pay me with a kiss?"

"Don't mind if I do."

After they'd kissed for a bit, she pulled back and looked up into those eyes she wanted so much to look at the rest of her life. "I'd like to make you dinner tomorrow night."

"There's no need for that, not after you've worked all day. We can just grab something at the café."

"I don't mind. Please say you'll come."

He stared down at her for a moment before

nodding. "Okay. I do have to work at the ranch tomorrow, but I can be here by six-thirty or seven. That okay?"

"Perfect."

So much excitement was pumping through Linnea after Owen left that she spent a huge chunk of the night setting up as much of her apartment as she could. When she finally fell into bed exhausted, she still didn't go immediately to sleep. Instead, she lay there imagining the dinner going so well that Owen would admit he loved her.

She tried not to let her hopes soar too high the next day as she decorated the table with a red, lacy cloth and white candles in silver holders. While the meal finished cooking, she fixed her hair and makeup and then hurriedly slipped into the new blue dress she'd bought at India's store and strappy silver heels. By the time six-thirty arrived, she was ready. She'd told Owen to come up the back stairs that led to the apartment's second-floor entrance. So as the minutes ticked toward seven o'clock, she found herself pacing to the back door to look out, then to the front window that overlooked Main Street to see if maybe he'd parked there instead.

As the top of the hour came and went, she started to wonder if something had happened at the ranch that had him running late. He could have called to tell her that, but she was trying not to be annoyed. She wanted this night to be perfect, and it wouldn't be if she was in a sour mood when he arrived. But when twenty more minutes passed with no sign of him and no call, she decided to call the ranch.

After several rings, Owen's dad answered.

"Hey, it's Linnea. Is Owen around?"

"No, hon. He left for a meeting a while ago."

A meeting?

"Oh."

"I'd tell you to try his cell, but he rushed out

of here so fast he forgot and left it here. Can I give him a message when he gets home?"

"No, that's okay. I'll catch him later." When she ended the call, she sank down onto one of the kitchen chairs. He'd scheduled a meeting for the same time as their dinner plans? Or at least close enough that it had torpedoed their evening.

She tried not to be hurt, did her best not to think she'd been a fool yet again. She'd tried so hard to avoid falling for another man, not to push Owen toward something he didn't want. She honestly believed she'd done everything right this time, but here she sat, all dressed up and with a meal growing cold and past its prime.

With a determined shake of her head, she stood and strode over to where she'd set up her bedroom area. Her movements were jerky and angry as she pulled off the dress and heels and exchanged them for shorts, a T-shirt and running shoes. After binding her hair into a pony-tail, she headed down the back stairs for a run. She needed to burn off the anger so she could refocus her efforts on the store and deriving her happiness from her new venture and her friendships. If the universe was telling her she was supposed to be alone, she was getting the message loud and clear.

Linnea ran up and down several streets be-hind her apartment before finally meeting back up with Main Street at the opposite end of the downtown business district. She nearly tripped over her own feet when she spotted Owen's truck sitting in front of La Cantina. She just stood there for several seconds staring, finally realizing that Owen was probably inside with whomever he'd left the ranch to meet. Though she was sweaty and not at all dressed appropri-ately to go inside the restaurant, curiosity got the better of her.

As she walked toward the front door of the

restaurant, she told herself she would simply satisfy that curiosity, then go home and map out how she was going to approach the next few days of preparing her business for its eventual opening.

The hostess was seating another couple when Linnea walked in, so she took the opportunity to poke her head into the main part of the restaurant and look around. The moment her gaze landed on Owen sitting across from a stunning brunette, it felt as if she took a punch to her heart. As if to make things worse, the brunette laughed and Owen smiled in response. Nausea welled up inside Linnea as she took a couple of steps backward.

"Can I help you?"

A moment crawled by before Linnea realized the hostess had returned and was looking at her with a warm smile. But as she stared at the young woman, the smile faded to be replaced with a look of concern.

"Are you okay, ma'am?"

Linnea took another shaky step backward before finally finding a response. "I'm fine."

It was a lie, and that much was probably obvious as she flew out the front door, nearly colliding with an elderly couple. She tossed out an apology but didn't slow down as she skirted them and hurried toward her new home. Somehow she managed to hold the tears at bay until she climbed the back steps and nearly fell into her apartment. Once she was inside, however, they wouldn't be denied any longer. She made her way to the bed and curled up into a ball next to the blue dress still lying there. Angry that she'd let herself get hurt again, she used her fist to punch the dress and everything it represented as her tears streaked down to dampen her pillow. She'd hoped to share that pillow with Owen tonight, but he was obviously going to lay his head down elsewhere.

OWEN WAS GROWING more fidgety by the moment, and he wasn't a fidgety guy by nature. But he was already really late for his dinner with Linnea, and he'd been so excited and anxious when he left the house that he'd forgotten his phone, so he couldn't even text her. And on top of being so chatty he thought she might make his head explode, Amber Roberts was a big flirt. For the past hour and a half, he'd had to maneuver his way around her obvious attempts to let him know she was interested in more than possibly buying the two horses he'd trained for barrel racing. He could straight-up tell her that he was involved with someone else, but he didn't want to do or say anything that would jeopardize the sale of the horses, because he needed that money.

Amber leaned on the table, giving him a good view of her cleavage. "So, what do you say we go to the music hall after this?"

He jerked his eyes upward toward her face.

"I'm sorry, but I can't." *Please don't let this kill the sale.* "I've already got other plans." If Linnea didn't beat him over the head with a skillet the moment she saw him. She didn't deserve being left hanging like this, not after everything she'd been through.

Amber pouted. "Just my luck. Well, then, I guess we better finalize our business."

About damn time. He kept his thoughts hidden behind a friendly smile as Amber pulled out her checkbook and wrote him a check for the amount of the two animals.

"I'll come by tomorrow morning and pick them up," she said as she extended the check to him.

That check might not make him as rich as Michael Benson, but it certainly was a step in the right direction. He couldn't help but think that this moment might not even have happened without Linnea showing the confidence she had in his training business.

When he finally extricated himself from Amber's presence five minutes later, he nearly ran to Linnea's apartment. But when he reached the top of the stairs, it was dark inside. And despite the fact that he knocked half a dozen times, she didn't come to the door. He turned and scanned the area behind the building, but he didn't see her there, either, only her car. Worry settled in his stomach, and it stayed there as he drove around town to see if she was out walking. It only increased as he drove back to the ranch. Had she been wrong about Michael leaving her alone? Or was she just avoiding him?

His dad wandered out of the laundry room with an overflowing basket of clean clothes. "Hey, did you talk to Linnea?"

"No, did she call?"

"Yeah, good while ago."

"Did she sound okay?"

"Sounded normal to me. Just said she'd catch you later. Is something wrong?"

Owen shook his head. "I hope not."

But as he called her and then texted, getting no response to either, he had to wonder if he'd royally screwed up with the first woman he'd loved in a very long time.

OWEN BARELY SLEPT with thoughts of Linnea and how he might have ruined everything battering against his skull all night. He was up early the next morning to put the next phase of his plan in motion, hoping it wasn't all in vain. By midmorning, he was parking on Main Street. He didn't think he'd ever been so nervous as he got out of his truck and walked the short distance to Linnea's store. The first thing he noticed was a stack of boxes shoved against the wall. Evidently, the first of her stock had arrived. He imagined how exciting that had to be for her.

But then he saw her sitting in a chair in the middle of the space, and she looked anything but excited. In fact, she looked so sad and alone that it broke his heart. And he had no doubt he'd put that look on her face. He hoped that within a few minutes he could replace that expression with a very different one.

With a deep breath, he pulled open the door and stepped inside. When she glanced at him, he felt the apology come tumbling out of him. "I'm so sorry about last night. I didn't have my phone so I could let you know I was running late."

She shrugged. "Whatever."

"I have a reason."

"Yes, I know. I saw your reason. She's very pretty."

Damn, she'd seen him with Amber. "It wasn't what you think."

She snorted. "I wonder how many times men have used that exact sentence throughout history."

He heard the hurt in her voice, and he could

kick himself for being the cause even if he hadn't meant to be.

"You only saw part of the reason. The woman you saw me with is Amber Roberts, a barrel racer."

"Don't worry about it. I told you it was just a fling, right?"

It might have started out that way, but what was between them had ceased being a fling a long time ago, maybe even before they'd made love the first time. At least for him it had, as much as he'd fought that truth. And by the way she was treating him now, he had to believe he mattered to her, as well. Why else would she look so sad sitting in the middle of her new dream business one minute and acting as if she didn't care what he did the next?

"You're not just a fling to me, Lin."

She slowly turned her head to look at him, something shining in her eyes that he could only assume was hope mixed with wariness.

"I sold some horses to Amber so I could buy something for you." He closed the distance between them and then kneeled before her. With one hand, he caressed her cheek. "I know it's not been long since you were engaged to someone else, but I need you to know that I love you, Lin."

He heard her breath catch, which caused his pulse to pick up its pace. Taking it as a good sign, he reached into his shirt pocket and pulled out the black box holding the ring Chloe had helped him pick out. He held it in one hand while he opened the lid with the other.

Linnea gasped and brought one of her hands to her mouth as her eyes widened.

"If you don't like it, you can pick out another. But Chloe assured me you'd like this one."

Linnea reached out and ran her finger over the diamonds in the ring as if she was afraid it would disappear with her touch.

"You got this for me?"

He chuckled. "Who else would I get it for when you're the one I'm crazy in love with?"

She looked into his eyes then. "You are?"

"You sound so surprised."

"I'd hoped you might someday feel the same way that I do about you, but I couldn't have dreamed that day would come so soon."

"So I'm gathering that you wouldn't mind being your store's first client?"

There were tears shining in her eyes as she shook her head.

He slid the ring from the box and held it up. "In that case, Linnea Holland, will you marry me?"

She cupped his cheek with her palm and looked at him as if she couldn't believe she was so lucky. He'd never felt so incredible in his life. "Yes, Owen Brody, I will marry you."

He slipped the ring onto her finger, then pulled her into his arms as he stood. "I'm sorry about last night."

"I'll forgive you if you kiss me."

He smiled. "Done."

She felt so good, so right in his arms as they kissed. Finally, he had to pull away or he was going to carry her upstairs and spend the day making love to her. "I'm taking you out for dinner tonight, but I better go if either of us wants to get any work done today."

Linnea nodded. "Yeah. I need to get this business up and going before you change your mind."

Owen ran his thumb across her bottom lip. "I'm not going to change my mind, no matter how long it takes you."

"I'm going to hold you to that." She kissed him as though she'd been waiting her entire life to do so.

As he walked toward the door a few minutes later, he had a hard time not smiling like a fool.

"Hey, Owen."

He turned to face her.

"Thank you."

"For proposing?"

"For making me believe in fairy-tale endings again. After Michael, I thought maybe they didn't exist. Now I know I just wasn't looking in the right place."

He'd never been so touched by simple words, so much so that he strode back toward her and scooped her up into his arms and headed for the stairs to the apartment.

Linnea laughed. "I thought you had to go work."

"Screw work. I'm taking a vacation day."

She smiled at him as he climbed the stairs. "What are we going to do with an entire day?"

"I think you already know the answer to that question."

"Indeed, I do."

He liked hearing the words *I do* come out of her mouth. Though no one in Blue Falls save maybe Verona Charles would ever have believed it of him, Owen Brody was more than ready to be a married man. Of course, he was marrying the kindest, most beautiful woman in Texas. The woman he loved more than life itself.

* * * * *

MILLS & BOON®

Why shop at millsandboon.co.uk?

Each year, thousands of romance readers find their perfect read at millsandboon.co.uk. That's because we're passionate about bringing you the very best romantic fiction. Here are some of the advantages of shopping at www.millsandboon.co.uk:

* **Get new books first**—you'll be able to buy your favourite books one month before they hit the shops

* **Get exclusive discounts**—you'll also be able to buy our specially created monthly collections, with up to 50% off the RRP

* **Find your favourite authors**—latest news, interviews and new releases for all your favourite authors and series on our website, plus ideas for what to try next

* **Join in**—once you've bought your favourite books, don't forget to register with us to rate, review and join in the discussions

Visit **www.millsandboon.co.uk**
for all this and more today!